The Oak Hotel

The Chronicles of

Burnam Tau'roh

Book One

WalterKline

Also by Walter G. Klimczak

Falling in the Garden

This Place Only

My Forgotten Life

Blackberry Way

Praise for *Falling in the Garden*

"...a magical miracle... involving time travel and alternate dimensions. The story is tightly plotted, with the mystery building quickly and smoothly. (An) enjoyable journey. The best kind of science fiction: The science sows the seeds, but the story grows the garden."

–Kirkus Reviews

The Oak Hotel

The Chronicles of

Burnam Tau'roh

Book One

Walter G. Klimczak

Autumn Harbor Press

Atlanta, GA

The Oak Hotel

The Chronicles of Burnam Tau'roh

Book One

Autumn Harbor Press

May 2008

ISBN 978-0-6152-0160-3

For more information about Autumn Harbor books,
please visit our website @ www.autumnharbor.com

This book is dedicated to my children:

George Bailey
Walter Joseph
Margaret McKenna

"For ye shall be as an oak whose leaf fadeth..."

Isaiah 1:30

"They are beautiful in their peace, they are wise in their silence. They will stand after we are dust. They teach us, and we tend them."

Galeain ip Altiem MacDunelmor

O deliver me!
Twilight deep within the wood
Across the great void

The Pandiment of Travel

Contents

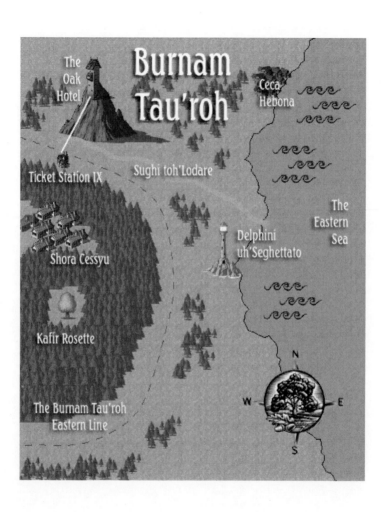

1. Five Notebooks

The soft ring of a brass bell from the front desk below filled the still air. In one hour, the Autumn Harbor library would close. Lincoln Torres sighed. He had been up and down the aisles all afternoon, but still could not find what he was searching for. He had even used a special pass (signed by both his parents and his fifth grade teacher) to explore the areas of the library restricted to those under the age of twelve. Not that he was looking for anything inappropriate. There just wasn't much about the history of Autumn Harbor in the children's literature section.

He'd been tempted to ask Ms. Ruttier, the librarian, for help, but decided against it for now. Lea Ruttier would have been the ideal person to aid in this quest, but he would have to talk to Kayleigh about it first.

Tucking himself into the most distant corner of the upper stacks, Lincoln shrugged off his backpack and pulled down the front zipper to retrieve a compact walkie-talkie. A birthday gift, this small yet powerful device had a range of almost five miles. Setting it to channel 3, he pressed the SEND button and said softly, "Kayleigh, are you there?"

After a brief pause and a snap of static, a soft voice replied: "Of course I'm here. Did you find anything?"

The voice on the other end belonged to his best friend, Kayleigh Lambert. She would have been right there by his side, aiding in the search, but was instead at home with a fever.

"I looked everywhere in the local history section. I spent an hour on the computer and found over twenty books in other areas, but nothing feels right. No mention of another town just like Autumn Harbor. If we only had a title…"

Of course, it always came down to this. They did not know the book's title.

About a month ago, Kayleigh had passed a note to Lincoln during school. The actual passing of the folded paper did not occur during class (which would have caused much gossip among the other students) but instead in the hallway just before the bell rang. While their math teacher, Mr. Tegeyo, chalked an assortment of shapes and equations on the front board, Lincoln pulled the note from his backpack and opened it inside chapter five of his text book.

Lincoln,

Mom and Dad need to sell my Grandparents' old house by Christmas. All the big stuff has to go, but Mom says I can look around and keep anything else I find. She even gave me an extra key to the back door this morning. Up for an adventure?

Kayleigh

Smiling, Lincoln refolded the note and tucked it away. Looking across the room to his right, he found Kayleigh smiling at him from her desk. She knew he couldn't resist an offer like this and he smiled back.

When school let out that afternoon, their adventure began. The old house on Oak Drive had been boarded up for years. Kayleigh had never met her Grandmother and was too young to remember her Grandfather. The few mental snapshots she *did* have of them were based on a blurry handful of crumpled photographs.

Upon entering the sleeping house, Kayleigh and Lincoln breathed in the dusty scent of discovery. Every corner promised something new and interesting. Each room was an uncharted land. By the end of the week, having gone to the house every day after school, they finally unearthed the treasure that would lead Lincoln to the library.

Hidden in a wooden soda crate was a stained, baker's box containing five notebooks, the personal journals of Kayleigh's Grandmother, Laura Corwin. They had spent the entire weekend reading through them. It was an amazing time, especially for Kayleigh. Here was a part of her past she knew nothing about—stories about her family that had been completely forgotten or never passed down.

"You know," Lincoln spoke into the inset microphone, "We could ask Ms. Ruttier for help. She knows more about Autumn Harbor than anyone."

A crackle. A pause. Kayleigh answered:

"You're right. Don't tell her too much, though, or she'll start asking questions."

"I'll go now. She just rang the bell and there's less than an hour left."

"Good luck. Bye!"

"Bye."

Pocketing the walkie-talkie and collecting himself, Lincoln made his way toward the stairs that opened up onto the lobby.

How exactly would he ask her? He couldn't just say, "A long time ago, Kayleigh's Grandmother found a magical book about a town like Autumn Harbor in your library. It may have killed her. Could you please help us find it?"

Reading the first four notebooks of the journal had been like stepping back in time. Laura Corwin had drawn an amazing picture of a much earlier Autumn Harbor. It wasn't until the last half of the fifth notebook that things began to get strange. Laura wrote about a book she had borrowed from the Autumn Harbor library. She explained that as she read and re-read the book, she began to dream about it. The places it spoke of were oddly similar to Autumn Harbor. Laura mentioned some of these places described within its pages. A railway and a gatehouse... A huge hotel on the top of a small mountain... A nearby sea... A tall, white lighthouse with paintings on the inside walls... In Laura's own words:

It's as if the author has been to this sister town of Autumn Harbor while dreaming, the mind drawing new boundaries and limits. The book is not fiction, though how can it possibly be real? Now, as I walk around my hometown, I can almost see what is not there. I fear telling anyone of this. Certainly they would think there is something wrong with me. Tonight I will tell my husband, Emil. I will tell him everything about the book and how it makes me feel. I only hope he understands.

There was but one more journal entry after this.

"Is there something you need help with, Lincoln?"

He jumped, not realizing that Ms. Ruttier was standing before him.

"Yes. Sorry. I was... wondering..."

"I'm glad to hear that. *Wondering* in a library is one of my favorite things to do, too." It was her smile that helped Lincoln to re-focus his thoughts. The librarian's silver hair absorbed the rich, late-afternoon sun rather than reflect it. It was if she soaked in the energy. Though she was probably the oldest person in the entire town, her eyes betrayed her years. There was great life there.

"Well," he began, "I'm looking for a book that someone borrowed once about a town that's almost like Autumn Harbor. I don't know the title, though. I've looked at every

Autumn Harbor book here hoping to find a clue, but haven't had any luck. I know that the book was in *this* library, though. A long time ago."

"It would probably be quicker if you can tell me who borrowed the book. I can search the records by that person's name."

"Then you'll know the exact name of the book," Lincoln finished.

Her wrinkled face smoothed and another smile passed over it.

"So?" she said, retrieving a pen and pad from behind the desk, "With what name shall we begin our search?"

"Laura Corwin," he said, almost expecting Ms. Ruttier to stop and react to the name; she didn't seem troubled at all. Printing the name on her pad, she moved from one end of a long desk to the other and sat down before a laptop. A golden bell with a worn, wooden handle sat beside it. Logging onto the computer, she looked up at Lincoln and explained, "A few years back, we had all of our old records converted into digital files. It was about time, too. We had boxes piling up in several back rooms as well as the basement and attic."

She typed and clicked her way through several menus before saying, "Okay, let's see what books Laura Corwin took out of our library."

Lincoln watched as a small, blue progress bar filled the screen. Above it were these words:

SEARCHING AH-BT DATABASE... PLEASE WAIT

A brief moment later, after the screen cleared, Lincoln found himself leaning forward expectantly.

LAURA CORWIN, 397B
The History of Burnam Tau'roh
OVERDUE, DELETED

"I understand *overdue*," Lincoln said, "but what about *deleted*?"

"It means the book was never returned and the title was deleted from the library catalog."

"Why didn't they just order another copy?"

"Well, the book could have been out of print. There are a number of reasons a library won't reorder a missing book."

"What do you think the reason was for this book?"

The librarian brought up a new page and typed the book's title into a blank field. After a brief pause for another search, a terse message replied:

YOUR SEARCH DID NOT MATCH ANY TITLES.
REFINE SEARCH?

Ms. Ruttier brought up several more search sites and on-line book catalogs. A search for *The History of Burnam Tau'roh* brought the same result each time. The book simply did not exist.

"Do you think the title was mistyped?" Lincoln asked. "It's kind of odd."

"It's possible, but unlikely. Even if it was, the book was still never returned." She tapped a few keys and a nearby printer came to life. When the sheet was deposited into the receiving tray, Ms. Ruttier handed it to him. It was a hardcopy of the search result data.

His skin tingling, Lincoln smiled and said, "I probably should have checked with you first. It would have saved me the whole afternoon. Thanks anyway." He turned and moved toward the exit.

"Good luck on your search, young man!" she called after him.

"Thanks," he said, moving out into the early evening with definite speed and direction.

2. The History of Burnam Tau'roh

ayleigh sat propped against a mass of pillows, surrounded by a frozen sea of books. On her lap was an open, three-ring binder. The pages were filled with details both she and Lincoln had uncovered while at her Grandparents' house. She believed that if there was a hint to the missing book's location, it would be found in one of the books from the old house.

While thoughtfully tapping a pen against the cover of a thick volume titled *Practical Lighthouse Upkeep and Repair*, Kayleigh jumped as the walkie-talkie crackled to life:

"You're not going to believe this. I found out the title of the book."

Silence.

"Lincoln, don't be cruel. Tell me."

"Sorry. It's called *The History of Burnam Tau'roh*."

He explained quickly how Ms. Ruttier had dug into the old records using Laura Corwin's name. Kayleigh was silent until the very end.

"So," she mused, "The book was never returned."

"It seems that way."

"Hmm…"

"I know what you're thinking. The book must be somewhere in your grandparents' house."

"Exactly."

"But you're sick and I wouldn't feel right going by myself."

Another pause.

"Okay," Kayleigh smiled. "I've got a plan. Can you come over for dinner tonight?"

"I guess… but you must be getting ready to eat pretty soon, no?"

She laughed.

"As far as my Mom is concerned, you have an open invitation for dinner, lunch, breakfast and any other family function. You know how much she loves you."

Lincoln felt an odd flutter in his stomach, but pushed it momentarily aside.

"I'll stop by my house and tell my Mom, then head on over to you."

"Great. See you in a bit."

After an oddly quiet lasagna dinner, Kayleigh and Lincoln met in the far corner of her living room.

"Okay, what's your plan?" Lincoln asked.

"I think this may be the first time we actually get in trouble for doing something that was my idea. *If* we get caught, that is."

"That's not a real happy way to introduce your plan."

"Don't worry. It's simple. We're going to go down in the basement to work on our Social Studies project."

"But we haven't even picked one out yet. And it won't be due until after Christmas break, anyway. That's over two months from now."

"My parents don't know that. Normally, I don't lie about stuff, so they won't have any reason to question it. Anyway, we'll sneak out through the back stairway and go to my Grandparents' house to have a look around. We might have a solid hour, but I don't want to push it any further than that."

"How can you be sure your parents won't come down to check on us?"

"That's the tricky part. I could say something like we're going to be video taping ourselves for the report and not to interrupt."

"Maybe..."

"C'mon. You go on downstairs and I'll tell my Mom and Dad what we're doing."

Ten minutes later, Kayleigh was outfitted in a thick, forest green sweater and Lincoln in a jacket with their school logo (a tiny, multi-colored bird with the words Autumn Harbor Hummingbirds) embroidered on the back. They moved quickly through the late October evening. Darkness cloaked them as they cut through several yards. The air was cool and smelled of all things autumn—smoky and thin. The slight hint of sea salt was there, too, blown across town from Autumn Harbor Bay.

Holding hands as they moved through a dense patch of trees and bushes, they came out upon the house that once belonged to Laura and Emil Corwin. As expected, all was dark and silent.

The key in Kayleigh's pocket actually worked in all three entrances of the home. They both decided, however, that the back door was probably their safest point of entry.

"I almost forgot," Kayleigh added as she slipped the key into the brass lock, "Didn't we leave two flashlights on the floor inside the last time we came?"

The flashlights were, indeed, still there and the beams were bright. Lincoln and Kayleigh moved as ghosts through the hallways and rooms until they reached the master bedroom on the second floor.

"Do you think it's hidden in here?" Lincoln asked.

"I'm not sure."

"What was your Grandmother's favorite room?"

"You know as much about her as I do. She did talk a lot about cooking and baking in the journals, though."

They soon found themselves exploring every drawer, cabinet and corner of the kitchen. Nothing above, in or under the silent freezer. Nothing in the oven.

"We're running out of time," Lincoln said. "We can always come back now that we know what we're looking for."

A heavy breath of wind pushed against the kitchen windows with the faint pop and snap of airborne debris.

Kayleigh stood in the center of the room, hands on her hips, chewing determinedly at her bottom lip.

"Do you remember what the last entry in the journal said?" she asked.

"Sure," Lincoln breathed, listening to the rising wind outside. "Well, not exactly. Something about an entrance, right?"

"I've read that last page about a hundred times. September 30th. I can almost hear her voice in the words, Lincoln. *I have discovered the entrance. Not sure what will happen. Forgive me, Emil, if I am unable to return.*"

"And wasn't that about the same time she died?"

"My Mom said that she went missing, but she also said Grandma died, too. I'm not sure what happened. But you know… if my Grandfather read that final entry, and he found the old book, then he probably did something with it."

"Like burn it?"

"I hope not."

"He might have hidden it somewhere on purpose, thinking it was dangerous. Or… kept it close by."

The wind pushed with even greater force and was joined by a spattering of thick, impatient raindrops.

Lincoln followed Kayleigh into the living room. She sat down on a long, tan couch and stared at the coffee table before her. Both she and Lincoln had rested here many times during their explorations, mostly for a lunch break or just to compare notes. The table was nondescript. It had no special carvings or embellishments. It was simply a solid, well-made dark wood table. On the top rested a small collection of books—large, square tomes you might find on any other living room coffee table. *Birds of North America. Lighthouses of the Eastern US. The Golden Age of Cinema.*

"We never looked at these books, did we?" she asked.

"Sure we did. Every time we sat down in here. I never really thought much about them."

Instinctively, she picked up the volume about Eastern US Lighthouses and held it up to Lincoln. Smiling, she slowly removed the brittle, paper cover from the book. It was with this action that Lincoln realized how loosely the cover fit. Turning the leather-bound book on its side, they both read the gold embossed letters:

The History of Burnam Tau'roh

"Let's get this back to your house. Quick," said Lincoln, already moving toward the back door. Kayleigh was right behind him, the book held tightly beneath her right arm.

A heavy roll of thunder caused them to stop just as they neared the back exit. The bass sound was, indeed, a gift from above for they both watched as the doorknob began to turn. Grabbing his arm, Kayleigh pulled Lincoln back toward her and they retraced their steps back into the living room, up the main flight of stairs and then into the master bedroom. Stopping, they listened as the door below thumped shut.

There were voices, too. At least two people, maybe three.

"The closet," they whispered together, then carefully crossed the hardwood floor. Closing the door gently behind them, Lincoln and Kayleigh crouched atop a pile of old fur coats and Lincoln switched on his flashlight.

"I don't think they know we're here," Kayleigh whispered.

"Why?" was his equally hushed question.

"They're not looking around. The voices haven't moved.

Listening, they both agreed that this was probably true.

"Then we're stuck here until they leave," Lincoln said.

"Do you think they know about… this?" Kayleigh asked, opening *The History of Burnam Tau'roh*.

The book, though in good condition, did appear to be quite old. Not ten or twenty years old, Lincoln thought. More like *hundreds* of years. Turning randomly from page to page, Kayleigh stopped and gently brushed her index finger across a run of words. "My God," she said, "This book was handwritten." The illustrations, as well, appeared to have been painted onto the thick, yellowed paper.

"I can see why this book was so important to your Grandma," Lincoln said. "It's beautiful."

Another page offered a series of paintings depicting a tall and beautiful building at the top of a steep cliff. The image sent a near electric shock through both of them, though neither would have been able to explain why.

Without warning, they heard a voice from outside the bedroom doorway.

"Search every room. Every closet. Look everywhere. The book is here somewhere." The voice was deep, warm and smooth. A man's voice.

One set of footsteps entered the room and Lincoln switched off the light. He felt Kayleigh's hand slip into his own and tighten painfully. He squeezed back. The footsteps moved slowly across the room just beyond the closet door. Back and forth, thoughtfully. Then, as they feared, toward them. In a panic, Kayleigh tried to slide the book beneath the pile of coats, but it slipped and snapped loudly on a bare patch of floor.

The footsteps outside the door stopped.

"Truman?" a woman's voice called out.

When Kayleigh picked the book up, it fell open to the final page. An unexpected light from inside the back cover filled the closet with a strong, powder blue glow.

"Truman!" the woman's voice was louder now.

"What the—?" Lincoln asked, but Kayleigh silenced him with a quick hush. The two best friends looked down at a thin, metallic disc that had been glued or taped to the back cover. Impossibly, a rectangular screen sat in its center. On this screen, much like that on a computer or PDA, was a menu with four buttons. All were labeled in some foreign language. The only one that made any sense was the one marked Burnam Tau'roh.

"What is it?" that smooth, male voice asked.

"There's someone or something in that closet," the woman said in a whisper.

Impulsively, Lincoln reached out and tapped the small button marked Burnam Tau'roh.

The screen cleared and asked:

INTERNAL POWER RESERVE LOW...
TRAVEL TO LAST ENTERED COORDINATES?

The doorknob began to turn as Kayleigh pressed the YES button that appeared beneath the question.

As the closet door opened, a blinding flash of light filled the small, enclosed space. Both Kayleigh and Lincoln caught their breath as terrifying static warmth filled their bodies. Perhaps they screamed. Maybe their bodies fell fifty or sixty feet straight down. It was entirely possible that all this and more occurred, but soon thereafter they knew of nothing.

There was only darkness.

3. The Oak Hotel

They awoke to the haunting sound of children singing. Sitting up, Lincoln's head brushed against something and he panicked, hands flying up to push away at whatever was there.

"We're in some sort of tent," Kayleigh whispered, feeling around for an opening.

A moment later, they were outside and standing in a pine forest at the base of a small mountain. A steep path about twenty feet from the tent curved upward into darkness. At the top of the hill, they watched in amazement as a glowing strip of light danced in the sky. The hazy ribbon undulated through a spectrum of colors, swimming like a ghostly fish. The singing that accompanied this event was equally as strange, as if a hundred young voices were telling the same story, but in different languages. The tones and harmonies were bent and warped by the swimming nature of the light. It was awesome and eerie at the same instant.

And then it was gone. As if someone had switched off the bizarre effect with an idle finger, all was dark and silent.

Standing shoulder to shoulder in the thickening darkness, the spell broken, they moved back into the tent and discovered two thick blankets and two flat, but soft pillows.

"Where's the book?" Lincoln asked.

"It's not here. I already looked for it. I don't think it came with us."

"Those people in the house probably have it. Are you okay?" Lincoln whispered.

"I feel like I'm dreaming. Is this real?"

"I think so. It feels real. This isn't Autumn Harbor, is it?"

"No, but we can't do much about anything right now. We'll probably need our strength in the morning so we should just go back to sleep."

Yawning, Lincoln did not argue. They snuggled back down into the heavy blankets and wondered again if it wasn't all just a dream. Five minutes later, they were both asleep.

The morning sunlight and the sound of chatting birds made the weird episode last night seem even more unreal. Standing outside the ball-shaped tent, Kayleigh and Lincoln surveyed their surroundings and decided they were definitely not in Autumn Harbor. For one thing, nearly all the trees in their home-town were oaks. It was one of those funny things that made Autumn Harbor famous. Here, they were surrounded entirely by fragrant, wispy pine trees. The forest floor, carpeted in soft pine needles, was more sand based than soil. Another strange thing they noted was that the trees were no taller than about six feet each. A young forest, Lincoln mused.

They agreed that they would need to be careful exploring their new surroundings. Climbing the upward slanting path, they hoped the view at the top offered a better idea of where they were. The climb wasn't too bad, but the crest of the path above never seemed to get any closer. It wasn't until slightly after noon when they reached the summit.

"Amazing," Lincoln breathed. "It's just like the drawing in that book." Pushing past the final few pines, they stood at the back side of an enormous structure. Constructed entirely of wood, the building swelled perhaps six or seven stories into the sky. A nearby cloud appeared to have caught temporarily against the steep, imposing roof. Moving closer, they both felt a palpable awe at this sight, but weren't sure why. Of course, they had seen buildings much taller, but none with as much character or demanding presence.

Against the back of the building, an evenly spaced zig-zag of stairs coursed upward, terminating at a door. There were many darkened windows, but no apparent watchful eyes. Kayleigh arrived at the wooden stairway first and gently set a sneaker upon it. She turned to look at Lincoln, who was still staring up at the windows.

When he realized that she was staring at him, he shrugged, "We might as well climb up."

"You don't have any weird feelings about this place, do you?" she asked.

Lincoln was usually the one who had *feelings* about things and Kayleigh normally listened to his odd premonitions. This time, Lincoln shook his head.

"If anything," he said, "this feels like a good place. It feels…"

"…like home." Kayleigh finished, unsure of her choice of words.

With that, they began their ascent, counting each step as they went. Not a single board on the long journey upward squeaked or popped. It was as if the entire building had been crafted from a single piece of wood. Reaching the top step, the tired, but nonetheless exhilarated children stood before an open wooden door. Sharing a puzzled look, they both asked the same question without words: Wasn't this door closed before we started up? And then an old, yet friendly voice:

"Well don't just stand out there. You must be tired from your long walk. Come on in!"

Smiling, they walked cautiously through the doorway. Immediately upon crossing the threshold, their senses were overpowered by a deluge of aromas. Fresh breads, meats and sweet things—apples and peaches? Down a dark hallway, they followed the mouth-watering trail and finally turned left into a large room.

"Please, come in!" a small woman said. Her muscled arms moved like machinery as she stirred the contents of a massive, gleaming copper pot. Pausing a moment, she reached over to a stone oven and pulled a long, worn paddle from the fire. Upon it rested two long loaves of steaming bread and a collection of small rolls. Setting the fresh bread on a table, she turned back to the pot and added pinches and shakes of various herbs at her disposal.

Kayleigh and Lincoln watched in wonder, unable to speak.

When the woman stopped, she pushed her hands roughly against the flour-coated front of her apron and smiled.

"I have less than twenty minutes before near thirty sailors take the sky car up here for lunch," she said breathlessly. The silver streaks in her thick, brown hair hinted at her age, but her eyes (clear and strong) told a different story. Not knowing what to say, they just stood there staring at her.

"Well, I'm sure you're hungry. Follow me," and she led them down a secondary hallway to a storage space with a round wooden table. Already on this table sat a loaf of bread, cheeses, fruit, sliced meat and a pitcher of some soft, amber liquid.

"Please, sit and eat. Relax. When the rush is over, I'll come back and we'll talk."

With this, the matronly woman bustled back toward the kitchen area and they listened as she muttered things like *fish* and *chowder* and *confounded potatoes*.

"She never told us her name, did she?" Kayleigh asked as she sat down at the table.

"No," Lincoln replied, sitting on a worn, wooden bench. It didn't occur to him until just then how ravenously starved he was. Dinner last night at Kayleigh's house felt like a week ago.

"You think this is all okay?" Kayleigh asked, looking over the mound of food.

"Right now," Lincoln said, "I don't care." He reached forward and helped himself to a slice of dark, crusty bread. Atop this, he placed a wedge of orange cheese and a thick cut of some type of roast. Smiling, he topped it with another slice of bread and bit into the makeshift sandwich. Not waiting to hear how good it was, Kayleigh followed his lead and they ate until they were fully sated. The pitcher held a cool liquid that tasted like something between slightly bitter tea and fruit nectar. They drank the entire jug.

As they finished, the sounds of many large and hungry men tumbled from down the hallway. Much laughter and good-natured shouting filled the air. Before long, the woman returned to them, pulled a wide stool over from against the wall and sat down.

"My, that feels good," she exhaled as if releasing a deep breath held for hours. "Okay, now for introductions. My name is Mona. Mona Tarok. I am the innkeeper here at the Oak Hotel."

Kayleigh and Lincoln introduced themselves.

"Thank you so much for all this food, Ms. Tarok," Kayleigh began, but before she could form a question, Mona interrupted.

"If you please, young lady, I'd rather you call me Mona."

Kayleigh smiled and spoke again, "Can I ask you a question, Mona?"

"Certainly," was her reply.

"Well," Kayleigh continued, "Could you please tell us where we are."

Mona's brow creased slightly and her gaze shifted between the two children.

"You see," Lincoln tried, "We're not from around here. We woke up in a tent at the bottom of this mountain and somehow found our way up here."

"We didn't go to sleep in that tent," Kayleigh added, "We just woke up in it."

"The place we come from," Lincoln finished, "is a town called Autumn Harbor."

Mona stood and walked slowly to the doorway. She turned back and said, "The name of this province is Burnam Tau'roh." She seemed to be deep in thought and stared intently at the floor.

"Are you alright, Mona?" Kayleigh asked.

Looking back at them, smiling again, the old woman said, "Yes. I believe that I am. I'd like to show you something, if you'll follow me?"

Standing, they followed her back to the main hallway and then to a wide stairway leading both up and down. About three floors down, they turned left. At the end of another hall, they stopped. Mona stood before a closed, wooden door. An odd collection of numbers and symbols had been burned neatly into the door at eye level:

61746f746820616e6e6578

Glancing around, Lincoln noticed that similar configurations labeled all the doors.

Mona reached out, turned the knob and pushed the door inward.

The room was dark. A large bed had been pushed into a recessed area to the left and a large dresser of some dark wood rested against the right wall. There was a ceramic basin and water pitcher, two chairs and a writing desk. There were no sharp corners or harsh contrasts. Everything here was smooth and rich and inviting.

Moving directly to the writing desk, Mona pulled open a shallow drawer and withdrew a sheet of paper. Turning toward them, she said, "This never made much sense to me until now."

She held the sheet out and it was Kayleigh who stepped forward to take it. Holding it up so that both she and Lincoln could read, they jumped slightly at what they saw. Written in a flowing, almost calligraphic script were the following words:

Link On and Kay Lee

Please come to me

My soul is captive

Ka Tolerates

Our destination

Hellward Kottabos

"About six months ago, a man came to this hotel. He had these awful fevers and woke up in the middle of the night shouting nonsense. I had a doctor come up, but he couldn't do much. Three days later, I came down to this room with some breakfast, but the man was gone. This note was left on the bed."

"You think that *Link On* and *Kay Lee* are us?" Lincoln asked.

Before Mona could answer, Kayleigh looked at him and said, "This is way too strange to be just a coincidence. But how could he know about us? And what do these other words mean?"

Mona shifted uneasily from foot to foot, then said, "The doctor said they reminded him of songs his Grandmother used to sing when he was a boy. Said she always spoke in a thick, de'Na dialect from a long time ago."

Turning to Lincoln, Kayleigh said, "We should tell her how we got here."

Lincoln nodded.

As they retold their story, Mona Tarok listened intently, soaking up every detail. When they mentioned that the name *Truman* had been spoken in her Grandparents' bedroom, Mona's eyes widened.

"The mayor of Burnam Tau'roh is a vile man named Truman Stitch," she said. "Both he and his sister, Sheenie, have been causing trouble here for quite some time now."

Later, after they all sat down to a less elaborate (though equally delicious) dinner, Lincoln and Kayleigh walked to the stairway at the back of the hotel and watched the sky turn from blue to purple to black.

"Do you think the mayor and his sister are the same people we heard on the other side of the closet door?" Lincoln asked.

"I have this really bad feeling they are," she whispered to the darkening sky. "I just wish I knew how deeply *we're* mixed up in all of this. And why."

4. The Burnam Tau'roh Eastern Line

Lincoln started awake. He thought he'd heard thunder, but the dark room around him was silent. Sitting up on the low, comfortable cot, he swung his legs around and leaned forward.

"Kayleigh," he whispered, but there was no reply. He strained to see in the near total darkness, but could not resolve even the cot he had fallen asleep on. Standing, taking short, cautious steps, Lincoln moved across the room to where he thought the door was.

The sound came again, this time to his wakeful ears. A loud, murderous boom. The crash was, indeed, as powerful as thunder, though more of metal and stone than electricity and ozone.

The door opened and a soft, blue light spilled into the room. Both Kayleigh and Mona were standing outside with anxious looks on their faces. Grabbing hold of his arm, Kayleigh pulled him out of the room and all three moved quickly, but silently down the hallway. Whenever Lincoln began to slow, trying to ask what was happening, Kayleigh tightened her grip and pulled him more insistently onward.

Reaching the large, front atrium, Mona stopped and turned to the expectant children.

"Mayor Stitch is here," she whispered quickly. "He asked if I've seen two children and he described you both perfectly. I lied, of course, but he's searching the hotel for you right now."

From somewhere above came the sound of heavy boots on hard wooden floors. There was no way of telling how high up they were.

"Here," Mona said, thrusting a small pouch into Kayleigh's hands. "I found these things hidden in that sick man's room. I don't know if they'll help or not, but take them."

A familiar voice echoed down a nearby hallway: "Mona Tarok, I require your presence!"

"Go, now!" she said and ushered them quickly to the front door. "SkyCarOne makes little noise on its way down to the train station. It's supposed to return to the lower base automatically, anyway, if left unattended for more than an hour. That hour is almost up, so there will be little questioning its movement."

"Mona Tarok!" Truman Stitch's voice repeated with impatience.

After two quick hugs, Mona closed the front door and turned to confront the Mayor of Burnam Tau'roh.

It was barely dawn.

Their first real view of Burnam Tau'roh was one of shifting shades of grey. Looking up behind them, Lincoln felt lightheaded contemplating the sheer height of the Oak Hotel. It was a living thing that weighed down upon them. *Go*, it seemed to say. *Your help is needed elsewhere.*

Kayleigh turned away from the huge structure and stared out across the edge of the cliff. The hazy view below was dizzying. Far to the left, in the remote distance, there appeared the blue hint of a sea. She recalled her Grandmother's words and agreed that there were some very odd similarities between this place and Autumn Harbor.

Lincoln, however, was focused on the moment. He moved forward and examined SkyCarOne. An enclosed metal vehicle that might accommodate between eight to ten people, it was connected to a taut length of cable that ran down from the cliff to a platform far below.

"You think this thing's safe" she asked him.

Walking over to the upper entry platform, Lincoln pushed gently against the cold metal hull of what looked like a miniature submarine. The entire assembly rocked slowly on the cable. He looked back over to Kayleigh and smiled. "I don't think we have much of a choice."

Together, they entered and secured the door behind them. Painted on the inside wall was a logo depicting the car and the words *SkyCarOne* in flowing, blue script. A simple control panel to the right of the door did not require explanation. There were two touch pads, one reading *Up* and the other *Down*.

Touching the Down pad, they tensed slightly, but relaxed as the vehicle began to slide silently downward. As the hotel behind them shrank, they listened, but heard nothing. No shouts of anger. No fists shaking madly in the air at their escape.

SkyCarOne moved steadily down. They could now appreciate how high up the Oak Hotel really was. It would have been the perfect place for a castle, Kayleigh imagined. The whole unreality of where they were and what was happening made this trivial fantasy seem entirely plausible.

Lincoln looked out over the land. A railroad track followed the edge of a great forest, disappearing in a slow arc to the east and west. At least he thought it was the east and west. The sky was lightening out toward his left, so he supposed that this was east. Who knows, he mused. There was no guarantee that the rules were the same here as back home.

The ride finally over, the odd vehicle hushed to a soft, uneventful stop. Opening the door, they stepped out onto a platform identical to the one at the top and secured the door behind them.

Lincoln followed Kayleigh through the light mist, not questioning her route. Crossing a pair of recessed train tracks, they moved to the left toward a dark shape. As they moved closer, a small building appeared in the mist.

"I wish we had more time with my Grandmother's book," Kayleigh said softly. "I'm sure I saw a sketch of this place in it."

Stopping before the structure, Lincoln read a small, engraved sign above a shuttered window:

Serving The Oak Hotel and all Burnam Tau'roh
Ticket Station IX

They moved toward a long wooden bench and sat. From their current vantage point, The Oak Hotel was lost in the soupy haze far above them. The train tracks disappeared to the left and right less than thirty feet from the landing.

"Let's see what's in here," Kayleigh began, reaching into the small sack to examine the items the strange man had left behind.

The first thing she pulled out was a tarnished brass coin. In her palm, it was slightly larger and a bit thicker than a half-dollar. One side held the picture of a tree and the other the image of a lighthouse. She handed it to Lincoln, who rubbed his thumb and index finger back and forth against it. He shrugged and slipped it into his jeans pocket.

The second object was a tiny glass bottle. It had been tinted so darkly that it appeared almost completely black. A slice of cork was tied around the neck of the bottle with a short length of white string. Kayleigh tapped on its side, but could detect nothing inside. She passed it to Lincoln, who pocketed it as well, not fearing it would break for its size and thickness.

The third and final item was a photograph. It showed a group of perhaps fifteen men standing before a forest of trees. They wore dark shirts with a blurred silver logo on the front. Each man held a long-handled axe over his shoulder. The expression worn on each of their faces reminded Lincoln of a group of miners about to descend into a dangerous chasm. Kayleigh turned the photo over and noticed something taped to the back of it.

"Weird," she said, peeling off two tickets.

"What are they for?" Lincoln asked.

Holding the small, blue tickets closer, Kayleigh read, *"Good for One Continuous Passage on the Burnam Tau'roh Eastern Line."*

"Great," Lincoln laughed, "All we need is the train and we can finally get away from this crazy Truman person."

As if on cue, the sound of a train whistle tore at the still, almost dream-like morning. Unable to determine from which direction it came, they stood and stared into opposite directions. The whistle, deep and breathy, came again. It was Lincoln that saw the old, blackened engine coalesce from the mist. They watched in awe as the massive train slowed to a strained stop before them. The initials BTEL on the cab door were barely legible under years of dust and grime. Great gusts of steam plumed from beneath the boiler, masking the sound of the station door opening from behind them.

"Hey!" a deep, raspy voice called out.

They spun around, Kayleigh dropping the empty sack. The man before them, dressed in dingy blue-and-white striped overalls, frowned through a long, unkempt salt and pepper beard.

"You should'a knocked. I was just having a bit of breakfast. You boarding?" His words were spoken as if his throat were filled with coarse gravel.

Lincoln's first reaction was to take a very large step back. The man's eyes offered neither warmth nor trust.

"Yes," Kayleigh managed. "We have tickets."

Hobbling forward, the stout man snatched the small rectangles from Kayleigh's fingers and held them up for inspection. It was then that they were both able to read the letters stitched across the front pocket of his overalls: Clyde Manrope.

"They're old, but they look in order," he coughed, then handed them back.

"Who do we give them to?" Kayleigh asked.

Clyde Manrope's lips twisted into what one might misread as a smile.

"You give 'em to good ol' BTEL Number Three and cross your fingers. She's not what she used to be before they changed her. Lately," and here he spat into a nearby patch of weedy grass, "No tellin' where she stops."

As he walked back toward the darkness inside the open station doorway, the train chuffed an impatient cloud of steam. Lincoln and Kayleigh turned and walked slowly toward the train's only passenger car. Climbing the grilled steps, they faced a closed door without handle or grip. To the right of the door sat a rectangle of smoked glass embedded in the steel. Inside the glass was an intricate network of dark lines. Giving Lincoln his ticket, Kayleigh pressed her own gently onto the panel.

Immediately, thin beams of light pulsed behind the glass and the tall door slid open with a loud, rusty squeal. Kayleigh walked in and turned to Lincoln. The door slid shut with a quick and dangerous finality. Panicked, Lincoln held his own ticket to the glass and watched with relief as the same light scanned the thick paper. When the door opened a second time, Lincoln jumped inside and without thinking took hold of Kayleigh's hand.

"It's a good thing my Dad isn't around. You've been holding my hand quite a bit lately," Kayleigh smiled.

With a tone that let her know he was speaking in all seriousness, Lincoln said, "If something happened to you, I don't know what—"

The sound of blasting steam jets caused them both to jump again. A soft and mellifluous voice from some hidden speaker said, "Please be seated."

Hands still locked, they stepped over to a padded bench and sat. At once, they noticed another panel inset on the wall before them. The soothing voice spoke again.

"What is your destination?"

Good question, Lincoln thought.

After a pause, the voice said, "Awaiting verbal or visual response."

"The picture," Kayleigh whispered, holding it up. Lincoln took it from her, stood and walked over to the glowing panel.

He hesitated.

"You might as well try it," Kayleigh said. "We don't have much else to go on."

So Lincoln held the photo up to the glass. They waited as the light jittered fitfully for a second or two. When the scan was complete, the train jumped slightly, then began to roll.

"I will take you as close to Te'hæra Thorn as I am able," the soft voice said, "Please relax and enjoy your ride."

"Te'hæra Thorn?" Lincoln asked, sitting back down. Kayleigh took the picture back and stared at each face.

"What is it?" he asked her.

"I don't know. There's something strange about this picture."

"Do you recognize one of those people?"

"No… but I feel that maybe I should."

Sitting back, they stared out the dusty passenger window, watching the landscape grow more wooded, listening to the steady *thicketa-thicketa-thicketa* of the tracks beneath them.

5. The Cinema

The train continued to move rhythmically over the tracks as the sun rose higher in the sky.

"When this is all over with, how are we supposed to get back home?" Lincoln asked, sitting now on a bench across the main aisle. They had explored the entire interior of the train, but found nothing of interest.

"I've been trying not to think of that," Kayleigh replied. She was sitting (eyes closed) with her head leaning against the wooden trim of the passenger window. "This Truman Stitch guy might know, though. If he was in my Grandparents' house when we crossed over, then he must know some way of going between this world and ours."

"He might have another book with one of those small screens," Lincoln added.

"That screen might be our only hope. Unless someone else here has one. We probably should have asked Mona."

"I hope she's not in any trouble back there because of us."

"I have a feeling she can take care of herself."

They leaned slightly to the left as the train turned right on the tracks.

The scanning pad glowed blue again as the gentle voice of the train spoke:

"Please gather your belongings as we will be stopping in less than five minutes."

Taking a risk, Lincoln asked aloud, "Um… Train? Can you tell us anything about Te'hæra Thorn?"

There was no response.

"What did that old man call it again? B-T-E-L? Bee-tell?"

"Oh, right," Lincoln smiled, "BTEL Number Three, tell us about Te'hæra Thorn."

The voice spoke matter-of-factly, "I know that the people in your photograph are from Te'hæra Thorn because there are two suns in the sky behind the men. This correlates with several factors and that led me to the only citizen in Burnam Tau'roh who has ever documented such a place. He is a sailor and is known as Shipmaster Creek. His last whereabouts are in the general location I am about to leave you."

Kayleigh and Lincoln had already taken out the photo and were scanning the sky behind the men. There were, indeed, two suns: one large and the other about half the size of the first.

"So you're taking us to Shipmaster Creek, not Te'hæra Thorn?" Kayleigh asked.

"Correct. I am taking you to the only known variable that will direct you to the desired location. This information is neither guaranteed nor endorsed by the Burnam Tau'roh Eastern Line," said the voice.

"What a strange computer," Lincoln breathed.

The voice altered slightly, speaking in an almost injured tone, "I am nothing so primitive as a computer."

The train slowed to a stop and the door slid open.

"Thanks, I guess," said Lincoln as he passed through the door and jumped the short distance to the ground below. Turning to help Kayleigh down, he frowned as he watched her move back toward the scanning pad. After a moment, Kayleigh exited the train and BTEL #3 was again on its way.

"What's wrong?" he asked.

"Nothing," was her reply.

"You sure?"

"Yeah, just thought I saw something on that screen, but it wasn't anything."

At first, they thought the train had made some kind of mistake. The woods surrounding them gave no clue as to where to go next. Upon closer inspection, Lincoln discovered the remains of a path between two aged pines. Holding hands again, they entered the path and moved slowly.

"How come you and I never held hands like this back in Autumn Harbor?" Kayleigh asked as they pushed through a dense area of vines.

Lincoln thought about it a moment, then replied, "Maybe because things were safe back home. Things are different here. I don't want to lose you."

Smiling, she said, "Well... whenever we do get back, I'm cool with this hand-holding thing, okay?"

No reply.

"Lincoln?"

Pulling her close, he whispered, "There's something up ahead."

"What is it?"

"I don't know, but it's a different color than the woods."

They picked their way cautiously through the thick groundcover, conscious of the sounds and movement around them. When they finally came out into a large clearing, they stopped and stared in awe.

"Wow," was all Lincoln could get out.

Before them were the remains of an old, forgotten town.

They stepped onto a weed-strewn road that may once have been Main Street. Small houses lined the road to the right and left. Most were single room cottages, similar to those that proliferated along the coast of small sea-side towns.

It was at this moment when they heard the deep tolling of a bell. The sound repeated and they stopped. It was coming from somewhere up ahead, toward the end of the road. When the ringing stopped, Lincoln said, "Did you count twelve? Kayleigh?"

Turning toward her, he noticed that she hadn't heard him. She was fully focused on one of the houses to her left.

"What's wrong?" he asked.

"Right there," she whispered. Lincoln tried to follow her line of sight, but couldn't figure out what had drawn her attention.

"That house there, the one with the blue door and shutters," her voice was deliberate and focused. "Black roof. Red brick stairs. Strange symbol on the door."

Searching, Lincoln found the house in question and stared hard at it. For ten seconds, he noticed nothing out of the ordinary. Then... *there it was!* Movement from the front window, as if someone had been peeking through parted curtains, then withdrew quickly.

"How in the world did you manage to see that?" he asked.

Still whispering, Kayleigh said, "I didn't see it at first. I heard it. Then I saw it."

"What did you hear?"

"I don't know. There were words, but they didn't make any sense."

She took two slow steps off the road toward the house before Lincoln grabbed hold of her arm and stopped her.

"Right," he said, "There is no way we're going over there. Look around. All these houses are falling apart. Half of the rooftops are caving in. The yards are overgrown. People haven't lived here for a very long time."

Coming out of her semi-trance, Kayleigh looked up at Lincoln and her eyes grew wide.

"What did you say?" her voice was now her own.

"Let's just find out what's at the end of this street."

Side by side, they continued a short distance down the ramshackle road. Before they reached the end, an odd building came into view.

"What *is* that?" Lincoln asked, almost laughing.

Upon closer inspection, the building they both thought might have been a church was much more than that. Yes, perhaps it had once been a church. It did have a tall steeple complete with a brass bell. A few upper windows were even peaked and tinted with stained-glass, but this is where the image of a church ended. Lining the first story wall were perhaps a dozen movie posters. They were set in ornate, dark wooden frames and backlit to showcase the advertising art. Above the double front doors hung a neon sign surrounded by blinking yellow lights: *CINEMA*.

Walking up to the posters, they stared in wonder. One showed a frenetic collage of faces, each with a black arrow tattooed on the left cheek. This movie was titled *The End of All Things Sacred*. Another poster was simply a spattering of dark blue paint and a scattered deck of Tarot Cards. This one was titled *My Sweet Marie*. And then there were a few posters that seemed entirely out of place: *It's A Wonderful Life*, *Somewhere in Time*, *Superman II*, and *The Color Purple*— movies from the world of Autumn Harbor rather than Burnam Tau'roh.

"Why don't you come in?" a rough voice asked, startling them both "I just started a new batch of popcorn." Standing in the now open doorway of the theater was a middle-aged man dressed in the manner of a seasoned sailor. His graying beard was a scruffy thing that clung in uneven patches to his face and neck.

"My name is Creek. If anyone around here remembers me, I'd probably go by Shipmaster Creek, but I've been on dry land for so long I no longer require the title." He stepped to the side of the doorway and held his hand up in a gracious motion of welcome.

When Lincoln and Kayleigh still hadn't moved forward, he looked up above the trees and offered a sly and mischievous grin. "The day is falling away, my young travelers. I must insist that my humble Cinema is a friendlier place than that empty town."

Turning back to the road they'd traveled, both noticed that lights now shone in the windows of many houses. A few doors, Lincoln discovered with a start, were sitting ajar.

"They aren't all bad," the man's rusty voice sliced unevenly through the onset of evening. "No, but a spare few are far worse than bad." His eyes were sparkling now. Kayleigh wasn't really certain how far they could trust his words.

Still, the odd gravity of the moment did not inspire bravery in the two misplaced wanderers. Hesitantly, they entered the Cinema and left the ghostly town behind them.

The foyer of the building was wide and led directly into the lobby. The interior was nearly identical to the Cineplex 7 in Autumn Harbor, only smaller. Lincoln couldn't help smiling when he breathed in the rich, buttery aroma of fresh popcorn. A long glass case, lit from within, held an array of candies. Some were familiar, such as M&Ms, Junior Mints and Snowcaps. Others, with names like RainBo Roll, Pop-Top-Taffy and Bubble Bitz, were unknown to them. A soda fountain, likewise, featured Sprite, Diet Pepsi and something called Cherry Ace.

The man walked with a slight limp to the other side of the counter. Setting large, worn hands on the spotless glass, he smiled, "What would you like?"

Both were very hungry. Still, they hesitated.

Not waiting for an answer, Creek turned and filled a large wax-lined tub with fresh popcorn and set it out for them. He also reached under the case and pulled out a box of Pop-Top-Taffy, adding, "This was my favorite when I was a boy. I can still remember getting an extra large box on my fifth birthday. I spent the entire day hiding it from imaginary Traders, making a bother of myself all around The Painted Lighthouse. Never heard the end of it from my father."

Thanking him, Lincoln took the popcorn and Kayleigh the candy. Creek turned and came back out to them. He led them over to one of many red velvet sofas. Sitting, the sailor rolled his head and the bones in his neck snapped like wet river stones. Then he just sat there, watching them.

"Okay," Kayleigh began, "We were told by a voice on a train that you were the only one who could help us find a place called Te'hæra Thorn."

Just then, a series of musical tones filled the air. Shipmaster Creek groaned, stood and walked over to an old telephone hanging on a nearby wall.

"Excuse me," he told them and picked up the receiver.

Kayleigh gave Lincoln a questioning look and pulled a long stick of wrapped taffy from the colorful box. Lincoln raised his eyebrows and shrugged. His popcorn remained untouched.

Creek returned to them.

"Young lady, did you say Te'hæra Thorn?"

"We need to get there. It's very important," she said.

Creek's eyes narrowed slightly.

"Getting there is the easy part, young lady. I can see you there by morning. The problem is getting back."

"What do you mean?" Lincoln asked.

"The route to Te'hæra Thorn is one way only."

A short silence filled the still theater.

"I don't want to seem rude, Sir," Kayleigh began, "But the sooner we get there, the better."

His shoulders slumped, "Then you won't stay for a movie? I'm going to show Superman II in about an hour. If you stay, you can even watch it with the Mayor."

"What?" Lincoln's voice asked in alarm.

"Well, not many people know about me and my theater here. They hid the road to Shora Cessyu a long time ago—and for good reason. This was long before I came along, though."

"But the Mayor…" Lincoln prodded.

"Mayor Stitch and I have what you might call an *arrangement*. I'm using a power supply that was outlawed over fifty years ago. Most everyone in Burnam Tau'roh uses it, though. Plus, some of these movies aren't strictly… legal. Traders still come through from time to time. More than a few laws were broken to get The Mayor's favorite things. He's seen Superman II nearly ten times already. He tends to look the other way for his *friends*… most of the time, anyway."

Grabbing Lincoln by the shoulder, Kayleigh lead him back toward the front exit. She turned and asked, "Is he on his way now?"

"Well... yes. Wait a minute. Are you two in some kind of trouble with Mayor Stitch?"

Alarms rang in their heads; they knew that leaving immediately was probably the wisest choice.

"Wait!" Creek said, stopping them just as they stepped onto the road that would take them back between the rows of now fully illuminated houses.

Kayleigh and Lincoln stopped, more because of the chill that twisted their spines in discovering the living lights now pouring through dozens of doors and windows. Impossibly bright lights.

"Look," Creek said quickly, "I'm not going to turn you in. I won't tell Stitch a thing. Promise."

They turned toward him and listened with an edge of suspicion.

"Whatever you do," he continued, "Don't go back through town. No telling what mood they're in, the old folks. Here, take this." He reached into his pocket and withdrew a slip of paper. "Go back around the Cinema and you'll find a path. Follow it until it ends. If you're sure you need to be in Te'hæra Thorn, that paper will help get you there."

In the distance, beyond the forgotten town of Shora Cessyu, came the lonely whistle of BTEL #3. When it blasted again a few seconds later, it was definitely louder.

"That would be *him*," Creek said dryly. "Go."

Without further encouragement, Lincoln pocketed the paper and they took off around the left side of the building. The dark path behind the Cinema was there as promised, waiting for them.

6. Kafír Rosette

They heard the train whistle only twice more, each time softer. There were no shouts of alarm and they were not, so far as they could tell, being followed. Still, Lincoln and Kayleigh kept their pace quick and wasted little time looking back.

When daylight no longer filtered down through the heavy tree cover, the path became much more difficult to see. They relied, instead, on the feel of the land beneath their feet. Eventually, they were forced to walk slowly and test the ground every few steps with their hands. Long hours later, exhausted, they stopped and felt their way to a large tree trunk. Snuggling down between its exposed, weathered roots, the full weight of the evening blanketed them.

"Did you get a chance to see what was on that piece of paper?" Kayleigh whispered.

Lincoln moved close so their foreheads were nearly touching.

"No," he replied, "I just shoved it in my pocket."

"A flashlight would be nice."

"I'd take a cold Pepsi."

"And a double-cheese pizza."

They laughed quietly together.

"Is it okay if I lean back on you?" Kayleigh asked, arching her sore back.

"I don't really smell that great right now."

"That's okay. You honestly can't be much worse than me."

Kayleigh rested slowly back against his left shoulder.

"I'm not hurting you, am I?" she asked.

"No, but tomorrow night when we have to sleep in the woods against a tree in total darkness, can we swap places?"

She swatted at his leg, "Don't get fresh with me, Mister."

Within five minutes, they had fallen into a deep sleep, lulled by the sound of their breathing.

"*Oh, such joy...*" a soft, hushed voice said.

Lincoln stirred, beginning to rise from night's ocean.

"*I can't believe you are here with me again...*"

Kayleigh heard the voice, too, but imagined she was still asleep and dreaming.

"*You now must wake, children of Earth.*"

At this, both Lincoln and Kayleigh sat quickly upright. Lincoln's back was knotted and his shoulder ached. Kayleigh found that she had little feeling in her right arm and her head buzzed with pain. Kneeling and then standing, they looked around. The dark forest they had fallen asleep in was no longer a foreboding unknown. Early sunlight spilled down through the higher branches and caught clouds of tiny gnats, dawn mist and floating eddies of dust. As they breathed deeply, the air smelled wonderful, as if they were drinking long swallows of cold, spring water.

Yet all was silent.

"You heard the voice?" Kayleigh asked.

Lincoln nodded, leaning into the morning to try and recapture it. A breeze brushed through their hair.

"Beautiful children of mine, listen please. Look up as well so that I may see your youthful eyes."

A mild shock pricked their skin as they turned to the same oak tree that had cradled them throughout the night. The trunk was at least twenty feet in diameter. The tree was simply enormous. Lincoln searched for a person hiding in the branches, but set this idea aside as the nearest limbs were over forty feet above them. He did notice an odd look on Kayleigh's face, though. Her eyes stared straight up into the higher canopy. Another breeze.

"Yes, dear one. Here I am. Do you see me?"

"See what?" Lincoln asked. All he saw was an ocean of leaves and branches.

"Lincoln," Kayleigh whispered, steeping beside him. "It's the tree. It's talking to us."

"How—?"

At that moment, a full wind blew through the woods. Through the endless combination of leaves brushing against one another in the anxious air, words were being created. It's like an immense and complex wind chime, Lincoln thought, playing a symphony of whispers and soft tones. He smiled and realized that he almost felt like crying. Here was something he had not expected. A miracle. It was something that should not be happening, yet it was.

The voice said. *"You are both so precious."*

"What… who are you?" Kayleigh asked.

"In the forgotten language, my name is Kafir Rosette. I am from the first of the singing oaks."

The breeze died down and they waited. A moment later, a long gust blew through and the tree continued, *"I have forgotten the name of my mother. I have never been taught to sing as she had. Have you brought me The Pandiment of Awakening so that I may learn?"*

Lincoln looked at Kayleigh. She was pointing to his pants pocket. "The note! Read it!"

"Oh, I forgot." He pulled out the paper and unfolded it. They were surprised to find only twelve words scrawled upon the crumpled paper. It was a poem, a haiku, which Lincoln read aloud:

"O Deliver Me,
"Twilight deep within the wood,
"Across the great void"

They waited. When the next breeze came, they heard the tree sigh with sadness, *"Oh, for sorrow, that is not the*

Pandiment of Awakening. They are the words that induce the Pandiment of Travel, or Feynman's Breach. I can now carry you anywhere a singing oak once stood if you would only ask."

Lincoln put the paper back in his pocket. "This is it," he said.

"Please take us to Te'hæra Thorn," Kayleigh told the tree.

Immediately, the thick and wrinkled bark before them began to shift. Long rifts in the trunk melded together to form a dark scab. It was this long bump that then split in two, showing a deeper layer beneath the bark. What Kayleigh and Lincoln saw in this sideway iris caused them both to feel dizzy. If they weren't so close to one another, they surely would have fallen. The simple act of peering into the opening caused their stomachs to twist.

"How is it possible?" Kayleigh asked.

It took a moment for Kafír Rosette to answer:

"Pandiments are keys. Some open doors to safety. Others offer the certain graces. I heard your Pandiment and created the great folding doorway. I learned this from my mother. Her roots once drew life in the Valley of the Oaks on the planet Te'hæra Thorn."

Lincoln took the first step toward the tree and the portal. Within the framed eye of knotted wood he watched a million shades of black and grey swirl in maddening geometries. This doorway terrified him. Turning to Kayleigh, he saw equal amounts of distrust and fear in her own eyes.

A breeze blew down from the sky. Kafir Rosette spoke now with insistence:

"I do not know how long I can maintain the breach, children. I am not a young oak. I must insist that you pass through now while I still have the strength. You are destined for great deeds."

Seeming to sense their hesitancy and confusion, the tree added, *"Do not worry. I promise to deliver you safely to the land of my ancestors."*

With this, Lincoln and Kayleigh moved toward the disorienting, silent storm of darkness.

"Good fortune to you both," Kafir said as they pushed their bodies through the slightly yielding, icy cold membrane.

Lincoln felt as if he was dreaming, though his mind was fully awake, lost to contemplate frozen darkness for endless hours; in one great lurch, he was finally dropped onto a soft patch of grass. His useless arms and legs did not allow for a graceful fall. His muscles no longer accepted direction from his brain. He felt their potential, but could not activate them.

Seconds later, he screamed as shafts of fire assaulted his body. Unable to stop the unending torrent of pain, blinded by the pure fury of it, Lincoln tried to center his attention on something else. Immediately, he found Kayleigh. Or, rather, an image of her face. Peaceful. Strong.

Eventually, the pain subsided, replaced by an intense and maddening pins-and-needle itch. When this, too, relented, Lincoln stood. Sweat coated his body and he shook as if in the deep throes of fever. Moving in sunlight, he knew that he was no longer in the forest. Before him, the landscape sat awash in a sleepy mixture of crimson and ginger. To his left lay a deep valley carpeted in grass and powdery clover. It appeared as if something sat down in the center of this depression, but he could not make it out. A rock, perhaps. Something dark.

Lincoln turned to his right. Resting on a rise of land was the most amazing spectacle he had ever seen. It was a city like nothing on Earth. Fashioned entirely of translucent, red quartz-like stone, hundreds of buildings, towers and other elaborate structures rose majestically into the air. The city was surrounded by a short wall of similar stone topped with an intricate network of some dark, shiny metal. It took him a moment to figure out what bothered him about this grand vision. It was simply this: the silence. Surely a collection of so many buildings and the mass of people who must live within the gated walls would contribute to at least a small amount of background noise. Yet there was nothing.

"Thank goodness," a voice said.

Lincoln spun around. Sitting on a bare patch of ground twenty feet behind him was Kayleigh. She was staring at him with a dazed and tired look. "I didn't know if you were ever going to make it through," she said.

"Let's not do that again, okay. Not any time soon, at least. That was simply too freaky. How long have you been sitting there?" Lincoln tried not to sound angry, but couldn't help it.

"Maybe four or five hours," Kayleigh replied. "When I passed through the tree and stepped out onto the grass, I was alone. The suns had just risen over the horizon. They're almost directly above us now."

Looking up, Lincoln noticed that there were indeed two suns in the sky. Looking again at Kayleigh, he shuddered as the last of the pain left his body.

"Are you better now?" she asked.

"Much," he said, and moved toward her.

"When you fell through, Lincoln, you hit the ground so hard. When I touched you, you screamed. I tried to…"

Her voice broke. She looked at him with a helplessness he'd never seen before.

"There was nothing you could have done," he told her, putting his arms around her and holding tight. "It just had to pass. It was horrible. How long did it last for you?"

She said nothing. Her frown twisted with a vein of regret. "When I stepped through, I felt nothing."

"Why?"

"I don't know."

Lincoln took a few unsure steps toward the city and stopped.

"Did you go to that city while you were waiting?" he asked.

"No. I was afraid that you might come through and I wouldn't be here. Besides, it gives me the creeps."

"The city?"

"No. That thing down in the valley."

Turning his attention to the left, Lincoln squinted to resolve the dark object far below.

"What is it anyway," he asked. "A rock?"

"I think it's… a tree," she whispered and immediately wished she hadn't. A shudder passed through her body and rocked her so violently she almost collapsed to the ground.

Steadying herself, Kayleigh closed the ten foot distance between herself and Lincoln and squeezed his forearm tightly.

"Something bad is going to happen," she said. "We need to get to that red city. Now."

7. Te'hæra Thorn

On their walk toward the front entryway of the city, Lincoln noticed Kayleigh's attention move back down the hill toward that odd, dark blur. Whatever it was, it definitely bothered her.

"What makes you think it's a tree?" he asked.

She didn't answer at first, though he could tell that her pace toward the city quickened. "It just kind of came to me like remembering a bad dream. I don't know why. I don't want to be anywhere near it."

"You said something bad was going to happen..." he prodded.

"It's either going to happen or it's happening right now," she offered cryptically.

"And this is just coming to you the same way as the tree?"

Not stopping, she turned and threw a very un-Kayleigh like look at him. It said, *"Don't push me, Lincoln. I know I'm acting weird, but get over it."* The fact that Kayleigh had traveled through the tree so easily told Lincoln that something was up. It had taken him a few hours longer to arrive in Te'hæra Thorn—and with a great deal more physical pain, too. The reason wasn't clear, but there had to be a reason.

They slowed as they reached the crest of the hill, aware of the lack of sound a typical city might create. It was not this, however, that caused them to finally stop. The front gate, a tall and elaborate affair, stood wide open. Nothing was locked or secured.

A breeze pushed through the open area, brushing insistently against them as they stood and stared.

"I thought there would be tons of trees here. Like the one back in the woods," Lincoln said softly.

"You mean Kafir?" Kayleigh asked.

"Yes. Didn't it say that—"

"*She*. Kafír is a *she*."

"Okay, fine. Didn't *she* say that she could carry us anywhere a singing oak once stood?"

Kayleigh nodded. "That's true."

"So there must have once been a singing oak where we came out."

Kayleigh turned to face the empty valley at her back. The dark form that caused her skin to crawl was now hidden behind the mound of the nearest hill. She concentrated now on the shape of the great valley. Rectangular. Nearly symmetrical. Again, she felt that something was out of place. Or, perhaps, *mis*placed.

"You know what," Lincoln began, "Isn't it strange that Autumn Harbor has so many oak trees."

Kayleigh turned to face him with wide eyes. "Over 90 percent of all the trees in our town are oaks. It's Autumn Harbor's claim to fame."

"We even have that crazy Oak Festival in town every September. There's got to be some kind of connection."

For the first time since they arrived, Kayleigh smiled. It was a small smile to be sure (curling slyly at the left corner of her lips) but it was there.

"Can I see that first note again?" she asked.

Lincoln pulled it from his pocket and handed it to her. Unfolding it, she scanned the writing once more:

Link On and Kay Lee

Please come to me

My soul is captive

Ka Tolerates

Our destination

Hellward Kottabos

"Before we even went through that book in my Grandparents' house," Kayleigh began, her voice electrified, "someone here knew about us. We're connected to these two worlds."

"The connection you speak of runs deeper than you might think," a deep, aged voice spoke from behind them.

Turning back to the city, Lincoln and Kayleigh faced an extremely tall, older man. His face had been etched deeply by the miles of years. His hair, white and reaching down past the middle of his back, was held in check by a silver clip. His mouth formed into what appeared to be a smile.

A horrid, sickening howl bleated over the hills behind them. Instinctively, Kayleigh and Lincoln ducked and covered their heads. The sound echoed in their minds like the most unwelcome memory of a dream best forgotten. They looked back up at the man and found that his expression was now grave.

"It grows restless. Come," he said, turning, "There is much we need to discuss."

He led them down the center of the city. Getting a closer view of the structures in no way diminished their glory. Lincoln noticed and pointed out to Kayleigh that the rose-quartz surfaces around them had been carved in the greatest of detail. One tower had been inscribed in an unending spiral of flowers. A shorter building displayed etchings of exotic creatures.

"What do all these pictures on the buildings mean?" Kayleigh couldn't help but ask.

Without turning, the man cleared his throat and spoke with mild irritation, "The work of children over ten millennia ago. There are as many theories to their individual meanings as decorations themselves."

They spoke no more until reaching a slender tower near what Lincoln guessed might be the center of the city. Here, the old man turned and attempted that smile again. His voice, however, belied his impatience:

"I wish we could have met under more cheerful circumstances. I'm rather shocked you're even here."

"Before we go anywhere else," Kayleigh began in a stern tone, "You will answer a few questions."

At first, Lincoln smiled at her raw nerve, then allowed himself to fill up on her well-placed anger.

The man's face did not show any reaction to her query.

She continued, "I want to know exactly where we are. What is this place? What is that horrible thing in the valley? Why did it hurt Lincoln to travel here and not me? And who are you?"

Lincoln took a chance and reached out to set his hand on her shoulder. He hoped to offer some of his own strength.

"If I answer your questions, will you follow me into this tower?" the man asked.

Kayleigh nodded.

"Very well then. You are on Te'hæra Thorn, the fourth planet in a binary star system unimaginably far from your own Earth. The name of this once great city is Kana Hove. That *thing* in the valley is Ka Tolerates, an oak tree. It is, as you have stated, quite horrible. Lincoln," he paused, "The reason behind the pain and the length of time it took you to travel between worlds is this: you are not of royal blood."

"But I don't—" Kayleigh said, then stopped. "Oh, no. You're not going to tell me—"

"Yes," he continued, "Kayleigh Kell-Korai Lambert, you are of royal blood and a princess. Your family traces back a very distinguished lineage."

Staring at him, she did not know how much of this she was prepared to believe.

"I don't have a middle name," she said. "And I can't honestly imagine my mother giving some goofy name like *Kell-Korai*."

Bristling, the man straightened and his lips pressed into a thin line. "Young lady, I would ask that you show respect for a name that has been passed down through countless generations. A name you share with women who have done many great things."

"How can I respect something I don't understand?" she shot back.

"That is why you must now follow me into the Tower of Quercus."

"You still haven't told us who you are," Kayleigh finished.

Lincoln watched as the elder man's eyes sparkled. His voice rose slightly in a playful (almost hurt) tone:

"I was hoping you might recognize your own Grandfather, Kayleigh."

As if on cue, the air grew still.

"But… you died," Kayleigh said softly.

Emil Corwin stepped back and placed his hands gently on her shoulders.

"My dear, there is a much easier way to explain this all to you, but we haven't much time. Will you come with me now? Both of you?"

Kayleigh and Lincoln followed him inside the tower. The interior was much like the curve of the outer wall, carved in an unending array of symbols and pictograms. At the far end of the room sat a small door with an acorn engraved upon it. Emil led them to the center of the room and sat before a circular depression in the floor. Not knowing what else to do, they sat down beside him.

Resting in the recessed stone bowl before them were what appeared to be millions of tiny glass beads. Kayleigh watched her grandfather as he closed his eyes and gently rested both hands on his crossed legs, palms up.

For nearly a minute, nothing happened. Lincoln was about to speak, but Kayleigh reached out and touched his shoulder, shaking her head *no*. Lincoln nodded.

A moment after this brief exchange, a sudden sound caused their skin to chill—the sound of ice being stirred in tub of slushy water. Dire preparation for a fevered body.

The culprit was, in fact, the mass of incredibly small, transparent beads. They moved in a foamy, chaotic manner inside the bowl. Misty water at the bottom of a waterfall, Lincoln thought. Kayleigh recalled the soft hiss left behind when an ocean wave pulled back from the shoreline.

"I will need to take you back many thousands of years," Emil explained with quiet determination.

In one breathtaking movement, the beads exploded into the air, stopping a few feet above them. As if linked together, they grew first blurry, then dark. No longer were there separate bits floating before them, but rather a single, three dimensional blanket.

"Let the show begin," Lincoln whispered.

8. Valley of the Oaks

As if drawn into a movie while sitting in a darkened theater, Lincoln and Kayleigh watched as the beads manipulated light to create the image of a beautiful blue-green planet floating in the darkness of space. It resembled Earth, though the shape and arrangement of its many continents were different.

"Our ancestors chose this planet for its lack of civilization. We knew of this city and learned that it had been abandoned for over two thousand years. It would be, we imagined, the ideal place to continue our inward search for peace. The world we left behind was a brutal one. Its leaders were selfish and power hungry. They feared us and meant to destroy us. We were healers, our minds open to the mysteries of the universe. Our escape was a tenuous one. Of the tens of thousands that tried to leave our world, only hundreds made it.

Here, the image of a black, horse-shoe shaped ship raced across the edge of space; it sparked briefly as it scratched the upper reaches of the planet's atmosphere.

"We took extreme care choosing our safe refuge, hiding ourselves well. There was, however, one great surprise awaiting us. We did not want to impose ourselves on a planet that already held intelligent life. From all of our scans, we knew that Te'hæra Thorn conformed to this criteria. Our lifestyles would be simple, we proposed. What we took from the land in the form of food, we would gratefully give back."

The planet faded, replaced by the image of a great tree.

"And then we discovered the de'Malange. In appearance, they looked like simple oak trees. More intelligent than any other life form we knew of, they became our mentors. They taught us many things, helping us along a renewed course of spiritual awareness. About five hundred years after our arrival, they grew comfortable enough to teach us the Pandiments, poems which held great power over the physical world. There were ten original Pandiments, though in time we began to collaborate and helped to create new ones. It was a glorious time of learning and rebirth."

"We met an oak like this," Kayleigh said softly. "Kafir Rosette. She said she was one of the singing oaks."

The image of the oak tree before them morphed into a great forest of trees. A sea of leaves swelled and sighed in an unfelt wind.

"Kafir Rosette may well be the last of the de'Malange," Emil said. "And, yes, she was a singing oak. Her family once filled the center of the great valley below Kana Hove. I'm sure you noticed the empty field on your walk here."

Behind the trees in the image, an artificial sky began to brighten with dawn.

"Long ago, when the suns filled the sky and the morning breezes blew, the singing oaks would catch the light in their leaves and branches and create the most beautiful music. The Symphony of Dawn woke us each morning. At twilight, a cooler wind would work its way through the Valley of the Oaks and cause them to sing the mournful Symphony of Dusk. It was a time of deep introspection."

The image swirled to show a close up of one of the trees. The bark appeared strong, willing to withstand any imaginable natural threat.

"In the decades that followed, we felt a great swelling of united brotherhood. Something had changed, allowing our kind to work more closely and with less strife. After a time, the trees spoke to us and explained what they had done."

The spheres changed color quickly to show a cross-section of a tree trunk. The thick, central core contained a deep, green moving mass—its lifeblood, Lincoln guessed, as did Kayleigh. The rings around it were nearly white, but toward the end showed darkening orbits. The final few rings at the end were almost entirely black.

"They were taking our negative energy. Their power was far greater than we had guessed. By taking our worst thoughts and intentions away, they intended to help our spiritual quest. We were, of course, quite upset at what this might do to them. They explained that by dispersing all of our negative energy amongst themselves, no harm would come to them. And, so far as we could tell, no harm did come."

The light that fell through the tower's open doorway waned. Emil closed his fists and the collection of spheres fell back into the basin with a soft hiss. The old man opened his eyes and looked at them.

"I can probably guess what your next question will be," he said.

"Well, yeah," Lincoln said, "What happened to all the trees?"

"And all the people," Kayleigh added.

Standing, Emil nodded.

"Two very good questions, indeed," he said, and turned. They followed him across the room toward the closed door.

"More answers await us on the other side," the old man said softly. He reached out and pulled the door open, revealing stairs that led upward.

As they climbed, the steps twisted to the left and right, causing Kayleigh and Lincoln to feel as if the tower itself were swaying. Kayleigh tried to count the steps, but lost track somewhere around thirty. Her anger at this man, her *Grandfather*, grew stronger the further up they went.

"You know," Kayleigh began, already out of breath, "I was actually hoping I'd meet my Grandmother. Either here or in Burnam Tau'roh. It was kind of the whole reason behind us coming here. I never imagined I would find you."

No response from the man.

Lincoln cast a sidelong glance at Kayleigh.

"Maybe I should just come out and ask it, then," Kayleigh continued, her voice a bit more edgy. "Is my Grandmother still alive? She did travel through that book, right?"

Emil stopped and turned.

"You don't have the book with you?" he asked, eyebrows raised.

"No," Kayleigh said flatly.

"It kind of ran out of batteries," Lincoln added wryly.

"That book," Emil said contemptuously. He continued to climb the stairs, "I should have burned it when I had the chance."

Finally, they reached the final step and the top of the landing. One last door stood before them, the same engraved acorn burned into its center. Emil opened this door as well.

Expecting to find tables overflowing with arcane instruments and thick, dusty books stacked on canted shelves, Lincoln and Kayleigh were shocked that the room was virtually empty. The only item in the small, round space was a telescope.

Emil walked to the open window before the telescope and turned to face the children. "Your Grandmother, my dearest Laura, should never have seen that book. Never learned of Burnam Tau'roh. I fully admit my own fault in this matter. I failed her. I failed the de'Malange and my people."

"What did you do?" Lincoln asked. He could tell that Kayleigh's emotions were playing games with her more logical side.

"I simply woke up early one morning and felt violently ill. My head pounded and my chest was tight in dread. I stumbled outside and knew at once that something was horribly wrong. I soon discovered that everyone was gone. I was the only person left in Kana Hove. In a panic, I raced to the front of the city and ran to the trees. Certainly, they would be able to tell me what… what was wrong."

"The trees were gone, too, weren't they?" Kayleigh said.

"Gone?" Emil rasped, "Not simply gone, but taken. Stolen. The Valley of the Oaks was no more than the site of a massacre. While I slept, they came into the valley and cut them all down. The de'Malange were murdered. All that remained were lifeless stumps, moist with the remains of the morning dew. Thousands of my beloved oaks, all gone."

"Weren't there other trees, though?" Lincoln asked, "Other forests or valleys on this planet?"

Emil sighed, "Yes. Of course there were. The first thing I did was walk. I walked for days. I didn't realize how isolated we were in our city until I left its borders. We weren't interested in spreading out over our planet, so we left all but where we lived alone. I did locate other trees, but none so miraculous as the de'Malange in our valley."

"Wait a minute," Lincoln said, shaking his head. "You said your people came to this planet a long time ago, but you talk as if you were there. All these trees that were cut down... how long ago did that happen?"

Emil glanced over at Kayleigh. Lincoln looked at her, too, and noticed a cold smile play across her lips.

"How long, Grandfather?" she asked. "Fifty years ago? A hundred?"

Emil's face grew stern. He apparently did not appreciate being called out by this impetuous, young girl.

"The desecration of the Valley of Oaks occurred over a thousand years ago."

"How can you possibly be a thousand years old?" Lincoln blurted out.

"Oh, Lincoln, he's much older than that. Aren't you? A few thousand years on Te'hæra Thorn with the others. But what about before that, on your home planet?"

"How old I am has nothing to do with what I am telling you, child. I consider my age neither a blessing nor a curse. It is simply a part of who I am."

"Okay," Lincoln interrupted, trying to catch up, "So what happened between then and now?"

Letting a long, exasperated breath loose, the old man closed his eyes and refocused. "When I returned to Kana Hove, I discovered that one tree remained. I'm not sure how I missed her before, but there she stood, in a small cleft on the side of the hill near the western border of the valley. When we spoke, my sadness and confusion rushed out into her. I did not think of the amount of pain I caused this poor tree. She did not have the strength of her sisters to balance out the negative impact of my emotions. I felt so horrible that I stayed with her that night and all of the next three days. I tried my best to bring forward a more positive attitude, but it was useless. On the evening of the third day, a sound came from the city. I at once recognized it. It was The Symphony of Dawn! This time, however, it was not sung by trees. This time, a magnificent, multihued ribbon of light rose from Kana Hove and danced lazily in the darkening twilight. My heart was lifted and my ears drank in the music I missed so dearly.

"The remaining tree, however, did not share my excitement. This light, you must understand, was comprised of the souls of my people together with the life-force of the lost de'Malange. I still don't know why I was left behind, but while the oaks were being murdered, my brothers and sisters… changed. Their bodies underwent an incredible conversion into another state. Perhaps I was not yet ready.

Whatever the case, I watched helplessly as they rose into the early night sky. Before I could take another breath, they were gone. When I turned to the tree, I nearly screamed in alarm. She had shriveled to more than half her original size. Her bark was slimy and black. Her leaves had fallen away. *I am cursed to swallow all of your evil*, it said in a voice I'd never heard the de'Malange use before. It did could not speak with the wind through its leaves. It spoke directly to my soul. *They gave me my fill before they left. I had no idea you intruders kept so much evil hidden in your black hearts. I thought we had taken it all from you. I thought we had no secrets. I am Ka Tolerates and you are nothing but liars.*

Kayleigh shuddered, recalling that same name from Mona's note. Lincoln returned her knowing glance. Emil continued:

"In time, I no longer regarded this tree as a member of its former family. It became an unpleasant *it*. I shielded myself from its influence and kept my distance. If it had full access to my mind, I feared it might take full control."

"That thing we passed was this tree?" Lincoln asked.

"See for yourself, before all daylight is gone," Emil said, holding his hand out toward the telescope.

Lincoln went to it first. He did not adjust the dials, but stooped down and squinted into the eye piece. Immediately, he saw the texture of wet, black bark.

"Turn here to get a wider view," Emil said, directing Lincoln to a knob on his right.

Turning this knob, Lincoln's line of sight pulled away from the close-up image of the tree. As he did, he wished he hadn't. A knot of cold bile rose in his stomach. Ka Tolerates sat rooted on the hillside, but Lincoln found it difficult to think of it as a tree. It was stooped, its two main branches hunched over like thin, muscled arms. It rocked slowly to and fro, as if moving to some malevolent mantra. He was about to ask a question when the tree suddenly twisted. Its bark formed into the dark slits of eyes and a mouth appeared from a rotted area near the lower trunk.

The "eyes" of Ka Tolerates turned in a sudden spasm to stare straight at the watcher on the other side of the telescope. Lincoln choked on his own breath as he watched the ends of the tree's mouth moved upward in the sinister mockery of a smile. Its branch arms shot forward, lurching and falling in a manic fit. Although he could not hear for it was so far away, Lincoln could imagine all too well the sound of its branches rattling together, dry sticks clacking like old bones.

Lincoln stumbled backward from the telescope and tried to regain his breath.

"That tree is why I left. My home for thousands of years had turned into a place of horror."

"So you just came to Autumn Harbor and married my Grandmother," Kayleigh said matter-of-factly.

"I left this planet in an attempt to follow my people. I re-programmed one of our old ships to follow what faint traces the prismatic energy left behind. I never did find them, but I did find Earth. I grew to love your world and over the years became an integral part of it. And, yes, I met Laura Corwin and we were married. I wanted nothing more than to stay with her, though I knew that she would grow old and I would not."

"Where is Kayleigh's Grandmother now?" Lincoln asked.

"So far as I can guess, she is somewhere on de'Na. Possibly in Burnam Tau'roh. When she discovered the book, she grew obsessed with the thought of traveling to another world. I only wished she would have told me sooner. You've read her journals?"

Both children nodded.

"Why didn't you go after her?" Kayleigh asked.

"I tried. I spent years attempting to travel through the book. I still do not know where such advanced technology came from or how it connects your world to de'Na, but I was not allowed through. I remained to watch over your mother, Kayleigh. A few years after you were born, I decided I must return to Te'hæra Thorn."

"So you faked your death and left," Lincoln finished.

"Yes. I am not proud of how things turned out, but that is what happened. Since then, I have been watching Ka Tolerates. Lately, I fear that something horrible is going to happen."

Lincoln turned toward Kayleigh. "You said the same thing when we were walking up to the city."

Emil's eyes narrowed and he looked back at his granddaughter. "What caused you to say this?" he asked.

Kayleigh struggled to put her thoughts into words as Lincoln walked back over to the telescope.

"It happened in my heart," she said, "It felt like something was sick, a dream trying to get out. It doesn't make any sense."

"Sadly, I have felt the same thing. I believe that Ka Tolerates is trying to escape."

"It can't just pull up its roots and walk away, can it?" Kayleigh asked, horrified.

"No, of course not. It would need, I believe, a host. Someone would have to touch it, open its mind to it. It would then transfer its dark and cancerous soul into this unfortunate person."

"Well," Lincoln breathed, looking down through the telescope a second time. "This may not be good then."

Emil and Kayleigh walked over to him.

"What is it?" Kayleigh asked.

"There's someone out there," Lincoln replied tonelessly. "Walking straight toward that tree."

9. Ka Tolerates

"Please," Emil said, reaching out toward the telescope, "I must see who it is…"

Lincoln immediately stepped aside to let the older man look, but his foot accidentally caught on one of the tripod's legs. The instrument spun wildly in a quick circle. Both Kayleigh and her Grandfather reached out to grab it, but the instrument moved too quickly. Twisting out of reach, it landed on the solid floor with a blunt, sickening crack. The front lens was reduced to a brittle powder on the floor.

"If the person walking toward that tree is who I believe it is," Emil said, his voice cold and shocked, "We are all in more danger than I anticipated,"

"Who do you think it is?" Kayleigh asked hurriedly.

But her Grandfather just stood there, staring down at the broken telescope.

"Well?" Lincoln demanded. "Is it someone who used to live here?"

Emil did not respond.

"We've got to go down there and stop whoever it is," Lincoln said.

"No!" Emil shouted, pulled from his thoughts. "You'll never make it!"

"Is Truman Stitch down there?" Kayleigh asked.

"What do *you* know of such a man?" Emil asked, surprised.

"That's it," Lincoln said, moving quickly toward the door. "I'm not going to stand around listening to more stories while the world falls apart."

Kayleigh followed Lincoln and they raced down the stairs, pushing caution aside and taking the steps two at a time.

"It's too dangerous!" they heard Emil shout, his voice a warbled echo against the curved walls. "I need to… truth… about Stitch…"

Kayleigh almost slowed at these last words, but Lincoln managed to say, "No! Just go!" though he was already out of breath.

Powered by pure adrenaline, their bodies pushed by the fear of not making it in time, the trip from the top of the tower to the bottom took a full two minutes. To them, it felt like a freefall of ten or twenty seconds. In a blind rush, they sprinted across the main floor, avoided the pool of image beads and shot through the main door into the thickening twilight.

Immediately, they heard the sound of the screaming tree. Faint at first, the nightmarish screech and wail increased as they neared the main gate of Kana Hove.

By the time Lincoln passed through the open gate and made for the rise of the hill, Kayleigh had caught up with him. Together, they crested the hill and did not slow even as they noticed a shadowy figure standing no more than ten feet from the tree. Strangely, the shape remained still, facing them as they raced forward.

When they were about fifty feet away, Lincoln realized the true terror of Ka Tolerates. Braking suddenly, he felt something deep inside him roll and pivot. The evil tree, fueled by the hateful seeds that gave birth to it, seemed to hover in and out of reality. One moment, it looked like a charcoal sketch detailed by some demented, master artist. Changing, the tree pulsed into a writhing mass of eely, black lines that possessed only fleeting coherence. And then, it was simply a diminutive, wicked tree with a false mouth that screamed and burbled unknown obscenities. Counterfeit eyes, hidden by gnarled brows, knit together and stared with the blackness of the unending distance between stars. The tree rocked. And heaved. Lincoln nearly lost consciousness. He knew the ground was solid, though it felt as if he were standing on the thick waters of some phantom sea. The waves pulsed and pulled him closer, closer, *closer*…

If Kayleigh hadn't been holding onto his hand, he would be lost. Still, the thing tried to enter his mind and there was nothing he could do to stop such an unwanted intrusion.

Kayleigh, who had earlier been so distraught, was no longer affected by the tree. Her full attention remained focused on the man next to it.

It was Clyde Manrope, the strange stationmaster they'd met back in Burnam Tau'roh. Still wearing the blue and white striped bib overalls, the man pulled a soiled, white handkerchief from his front, breast pocket and wiped it roughly across his brow.

"Well, now," he said, "Didn't expect to be meeting you two here."

"We could say the same," Kayleigh said, moving slowly forward. Lincoln, wanting to stay as far back from the tree as possible, grudgingly kept a few paces behind her. How were they going to keep him from touching the tree? Even working together, getting the large man down would be near impossible.

"Are you sure you want to be coming that close?" Manrope asked.

Ignoring him, Kayleigh asked, "Why are you here?"

Just then, the air around the stationmaster shimmered, then crackled as if an electric current had been opened. The image of Clyde Manrope fell apart as the undoing of millions of tiny seams in some cosmic fabric. Standing in his place was the man they met in the Cinema. He was holding a crumpled box of Pop-Top-Taffy.

"Shipmaster Creek," Kayleigh whispered.

"I think you already know why I'm here," he said.

"Kayleigh, stop," Lincoln said in a pained voice. He was still following her. He wanted to stop, but couldn't. Couldn't leave her.

She did not turn to him, but she did stop.

"How much did your dear old Grandfather tell you?" Creek asked. He unwrapped a bit of taffy and pushed it slowly between his lips.

"What's going on?" Lincoln asked in a hushed tone.

"What's going on, Lincoln, is this," Creek began. "I have a mission to complete. A mission that has kept me from my homeland for far too long."

Again, the hazy after-image confetti snap and replacing Creek was a young man wearing a dark blue suit. His feet were bare and a pair of dark glasses framed his eyes.

"Again, I ask," he began, "How much has your Grandfather told you?"

Take off those glasses, thought Lincoln. Let us see your eyes.

"Truman!" a voice bellowed from behind them.

Kayleigh turned to see her Grandfather moving slowly down the hill. Behind him, the city of Kana Hove watched with silent, vacant eyes.

"Emil!" the young man shouted, smiling. "How nice to see you again!"

"How did you find Te'hæra Thorn?" Emil asked.

"Why, thanks to these resourceful children, it was just a hop, skip and a jump from my own little hometown on de'Na."

"You followed us the whole way?" Kayleigh asked.

"He tricked us," Lincoln added.

"I used you," Truman Stitch corrected.

Having closed the remaining distance, Emil moved past Lincoln, put an arm around his granddaughter and glared.

Truman cocked his head as he studied the older man, "Do not worry, I won't harm the girl. Besides, I have further use for her."

"You will not touch her!" Emil said, his firm grip on her shoulder tightening.

"Touch her? No. There is no need to. I do, however, have an extremely pressing urge to touch this tree."

Lincoln, eyes still glued to the hideous countenance of the tree, chilled as the false smile in the bark deepened. It shook its branch arms spasmodically at Truman Stitch. It knew that things were almost over.

"This is madness," Emil said, watching Truman walk closer to the tree. He was now within reach of the trunk. Ka Tolerates shivered in vulgar anticipation.

"You won't survive," Emil shouted. "It's too much. Ages of the most base and criminal of thoughts. There will be nothing left when this thing is through with you."

"We'll just have to wait a moment and see, then, old friend," Truman said, this time without the former mockery.

Just as Stitch reached out to place his flattened palm against the diseased trunk, Kayleigh felt her Grandfather push suddenly away from her toward Truman. He might actually have knocked Truman away, too, if it weren't for the tree. Ka Tolerates, seeing the rushed advance, barked a sickening cough, causing Truman to turn.

"No!" Kayleigh screamed, but could do nothing to stop it.

Stitch had just set his left hand on the slick bark of the tree. In one fluid movement, he raised his right hand to Emil Corwin and shouted a quick succession of words. Both Kayleigh and Lincoln guessed that if they had counted the syllables, it would have worked out to be a haiku. A *dark* Pandiment.

From Truman's fingers raced slithering lengths of dense smoke which quickly condensed into tight, rubbery bands. They wrapped cruelly around Emil, completing their work in efficient swings and tugs, pulling him in various directions at once. It happened with such speed, in fact, that there was nothing left of Emil when the bands fell apart except a fine dust that settled slowly to the grass below.

Kayleigh's throat constricted as she fell to her knees. Lincoln was there beside her, trying his best to hold her up.

Ka Tolerates took no notice of them. Instead, it reached down to Truman Stitch and wrapped its crackling branches around the man in an ominous embrace. Stitch looked up into the oily eye slits, seeing something meant only for him.

"Yes," he said in a choked voice, "Oh, yes."

What happened next felt like being blinded. Lincoln looked down the instant it began, but Kayleigh forced herself to stare at the spectacle. Tearing and ripping and deliquescing, the tree took itself apart. Each greasy piece from inside the bark floated in the air as if weighing nothing. Truman only stood there, taking deep, full breaths. With each inhalation, the insubstantial pieces filled his lungs. Kayleigh rested a hand on Lincoln, feeling him shake.

She thought about the man who was her Grandfather. She had just met him, but now he was gone. It was too much to process right now. Then she thought about Lincoln. If I could only send him back! I'm more involved in this than he is! It's my crazy family, isn't it?

A dark, living cloud now concealed both Ka Tolerates and Truman Stitch. It pulsed and throbbed, a living sickness.

And then it was over. All that remained of the tree lie on the charred grass—a mass of broken, splintered black wood. Stitch knelt before it, hunched over, his breathing loud and filled with hard, insectile sounds. He was barely moving.

"Lincoln," she said, combing her fingers through his hair as a mother would, "Lincoln, get up. Let's get out of here."

He stood beside her, but looked away from where the tree had been.

Together, they moved back toward Kana Hove. Kayleigh felt her muscles melt at the thought of lying down somewhere and recharging with a bit of sleep.

Then a voice asked, "Where are you going?"

Kayleigh and Lincoln turned.

Truman was no longer hunched over, but standing erect. His face was the same, but... the eyes belonged to the tree. The smile wasn't human, either. It belonged locked away.

"You belong to us now, girl," his voice cracked.

Raising a hand, the false Truman pointed at Kayleigh. Lincoln tensed, ready for anything, but there was simply no time to react. Not understanding how it was accomplished, Lincoln watched as a sphere of light surrounded her body. Just as he reached out, the sphere collapsed and a clap of thunder filled the air.

Lincoln fell to the ground.

Kayleigh was gone.

Smiling at Lincoln, Truman said darkly, "It would be very... unwise for you to try anything. You will only fail."

Stitch (or whatever he had now become) raised his hand and disappeared in the same manner.

Ears ringing, Lincoln stood. He was now as alone as Emil had once been. When his fractured mind allowed him to relive Kayleigh's face as it had been the second before she was taken away, he felt like collapsing to the ground again. He felt like screaming. He felt like giving up.

But he didn't.

10. Home

or days, Lincoln wandered the silent shell that was Kana Hove.

In a small courtyard behind the Tower of Quercus, he discovered a garden. There were vegetables—tomatoes, carrots, string beans among other unidentifiable varieties. There were also small-leafed plants that may have been herbs used for cooking or medicinal purposes. This oasis probably belonged to Emil. He took only small portions of the food he found there and ate only when his hunger would not relent. Water came from a small well less than a hundred feet from the garden. Lincoln could not imagine how the old man kept his sanity. The silence was unbearable. He tried talking to himself now and then, but this only made it worse.

Each evening, he walked back to where Kayleigh had been stolen away. Standing beside the sorry remains of the tree, his failure felt complete. His most unrealistic thoughts imagined Kayleigh reappearing there on the hill, deposited there by a familiar rush of light. This, of course, did not happen.

At the end of the third day, Lincoln recalled Emil speaking of a ship that had brought him to Te'hæra Thorn, from there to Earth and then back again. Was that same ship was still in Kana Hove? A small part of him warmed quickly to this idea. Still… how would he fly such a machine? In which direction would he pilot the ship if he did manage to start it? He wondered if there might be a way to learn all of this. Oddly, there wasn't a single book in the entire city. At least, none that he could find. At this thought, he heard Kayleigh's rational voice clearly in his mind. "Think about it, Lincoln. This is an advanced society. Information is probably stored electronically. And don't forget that books are made from paper. I don't think they'd cut down a de'Malange for paper."

Lincoln smiled. Though she was gone, the imagined sound of her voice calmed him. Dozing in and out of similar thoughts, Lincoln fell restlessly asleep. In the morning, the same question that haunted him throughout each day lifted him quickly through the shredded remains of sleep:

"How will I ever leave this place?"

It was strange hearing his own voice, which echoed flatly against the tower walls around him. He had been sleeping on the lowest floor of the Tower of Quercus. Of all Kana Hove, he had explored this tower the most. Still, he could uncover nothing more than the broken telescope at the top and the pool of beads below. Why wasn't there more *stuff*? His stomach begged for something to eat, but he pushed the cramped feeling aside. Walking over to the tiny glass beads, he knelt before the recessed circle in the same manner Emil had only days before. He set both hands palm-side up on his knees and closed his eyes.

Not knowing what else to do, he formed words in his mind and tried to sound as serious as possible. *Great spheres of glass, please show me where Kayleigh has been taken.*

As he expected, nothing happened. It wasn't, after all, a crystal ball.

He pushed harder and concentrated.

Create a picture of the place where Kayleigh is.

Again, nothing.

Deciding on something easier, he projected the following request:

Show me a picture of the de'Malange.

Lincoln jumped. The beads shot up into the air with raspy excitement. Agitated, they performed various acrobatics before settling into an organized dance.

Opening his eyes, making sure to keep his body still and relaxed, Lincoln watched as the spheres went from transparent to opaque and presented him with a moving image of the valley of the oaks. It was breathtaking.

Show me a picture of Emil Corwin.

The beads spun and colors blurred. In a moment, he was presented with a three-dimensional rendering of Kayleigh's grandfather, wearing the same clothing he wore when they first met. Taking a chance, Lincoln tried the following:

Show me a picture of Truman Stitch.

He was immediately presented with the face of the same man who had been following them through three different worlds. The man finally revealed to them in the dark blue suit and glasses.

And then Lincoln thought about Truman. About what he had become after touching the tree. This caused him to wonder about the power of the trees… and the Pandiments…

Show me a list of the Pandiments.

Before him scrolled a list of Pandiments. He read them as they sped quickly by: Pandiment of Awakening, Pandiment of Healing, Pandiment of Travel—

Stop! Lincoln thought. *Show me only the Pandiment of Travel.*

The area before him opened as if it were a book, offering the familiar haiku written on the slip of paper from Shipmaster Creek. Lincoln smiled. It was a long shot, but it just might work. He was amazed he hadn't thought of trying it earlier.

Standing, breaking the trance and his link, Lincoln watched the beads fall with a soft hush. Stretching his legs and arms, he decided to test his theory immediately. Glancing around one last time, he set the room and the cryptic symbols carved in the stone to memory.

Leaving the tower and then the city of Kana Hove, Lincoln felt a nervous anticipation fill him. A large part of him knew this would work. Still, a small part worried.

He passed through the main gate onto the hill and breathed in the fresh, morning air. By the time he walked down to the moldering remains of Ka Tolerates, he dropped to his knees.

Taking a deep breath, Lincoln brought the words to the front of his memory. In a soft, fearful voice, he closed his eyes and spoke the Pandiment of Travel:

"O Deliver Me,

"Twilight deep within the wood,

"Across the great void"

When he opened his eyes, he stared down at the carbonized wood.

Nothing happened... at first. As the seconds passed, a slick, black glimmer began to crawl up the center of the splinters and branches. This strange liquid movement grew larger and in time took the shape of an oval. A minute later, it was nearly the same size the portal had been on the trunk of Kafir Rosette.

Lincoln's eyes welled with tears. His mind and heart were an amalgam of sorrow, relief, anger and regret stirred with hope.

"Take me..." he began.

Where? He didn't know where Kayleigh was. Truman might be waiting for him back in Burnam Tau'roh. There really was only one place he could think of. A safe place to hide until he could decide what to do next.

"Take me home," he said, tasting the saltiness of his tears as they pooled at the corners of his mouth.

The portal seemed to hear his words and gave an almost human shiver of anticipation.

Lincoln lowered his head and crawled into the odd, yet beautiful swirl of darkness.

There was, again, a sense of time passing and great pain. This time, however, the agony didn't seem to last as long. When he finally passed through to the other side, Lincoln rolled out onto soft ground. When the monstrous headache eventually faded and his vision cleared, he could feel the cool, wet grass on his cheek and smell the salty tang of the ocean on the breeze. The sky above him was filled with stars. The land around him was pale, dusted by a full moon.

Lincoln stood and surveyed his surroundings. A tall building filled his view and his heart gave a jump. He was back behind the Oak Hotel!

But, no. The Oak Hotel had been much, much taller. It wasn't the Cinema, either.

Walking around the left side of the building, feeling as if each step were on a cloud, Lincoln stopped when he faced the front entrance of the Autumn Harbor Library.

He had done it. He had made it home.

Although it was probably well past midnight, the front door swung slowly open. Lincoln watched in stunned silence as a familiar person stood framed in the entryway.

"Come in quickly, Lincoln," Ms. Ruttier said, concern in her expression.

Still walking on that cloud, Lincoln did his best to hurry through the door. Immediately, the familiar smells of the library assaulted his senses. It was a good thing. This is *real*, he thought. He didn't understand how displaced he'd felt both in Burnam Tau'roh and Kana Hove until this moment. Part of his mind was telling him that it was only a dream. How could such things be true? What would he say to Ms. Ruttier? She'd never believe any of it! Still frowning, the librarian locked the door behind her and led him to a chair at one of the main desks in the center of the first floor.

Lincoln's shoulders relaxed as he leaned forward to rest his head against the desk. "It's so good to be back," he sighed sleepily, "I haven't felt safe like this in a long time."

"Oh, you're not safe, Lincoln," Lea Ruttier said quickly. "You're less safe here than on de'Na or Te'hæra Thorn."

Lincoln sat straight up; the muscles in his neck tensed and a familiar cold glaze covering his skin.

"What?" was all he could get past his dry lips.

"Both you and Kayleigh were reported missing a week ago. I can't explain how distraught your parents are."

"But… how do you—?" he stuttered.

Lea offered a small smile. "When Emil Corwin first arrived in Autumn Harbor, he met my father. This was quite some time ago. They soon became friends and eventually business partners. One thing they did was build this library. Years later, when Emil's wife disappeared through the book, he was never the same person. When my father died, I took his place and began to help Emil. We did a great deal of research on the book. Just before he decided to return to Te'hæra Thorn, he asked me to watch over both you and Kayleigh. We sat down and went over all the possible things that could happen, both good and bad, so I would know what to do. You and Kayleigh finding your way to Burnam Tau'roh was one possibility."

"But what do I have to do with all this, aside from being Kayleigh's friend? She's the one connected to these other worlds."

Lea smiled sadly. "Lincoln, I hate to be the one to tell you something your parents may not yet want you to know, but—"

"I know that I was adopted when I was a baby, if that's what you mean," he began, somewhat defensively.

Sighing with relief, the librarian continued, "Good. Well, then, that might make this a little easier. Lincoln, it's possible that you were born in Burnam Tau'roh. We were never able to track down your original parents nor do we know how you managed to arrive in Autumn Harbor. You were discovered in a small, abandoned boat by a local fisherman on the shore of Autumn Harbor Bay. He brought you to the police. What caught our attention was the fact that a book had been placed between the sheets that were wrapped carefully around you. It was a second copy of *The History of Burnam Tau'roh*."

"This all sounds like some kind of twisted fairy tale." Lincoln whispered, mostly to himself. Then, out loud, "Fine. I guess I can accept what you're saying. It's no stranger than what's already happened, but everything's gone wrong. Someone named Truman Stitch touched this horrible tree called Ka Tolerates and now he's some weird, super-evil thing. He killed Emil and took Kayleigh with him."

Lea's eyes clouded, but she did not look entirely surprised.

"Emil is gone?" she asked, though it wasn't a question that needed further confirmation.

"Emil told us many things," Lincoln added, "But he never had a chance to tell us about Truman Stitch."

The librarian sighed. "After Emil and the Pilgrims left their home planet for Te'hæra Thorn, two people were sent to find them and bring them back. Truman and his sister have been hunting without success for thousands of years. We believe that they're not allowed to return unless they bring the Pilgrims back. With Emil now gone, he might have no reason to return. This makes him much more dangerous."

"Emil said his people and the oaks turned into some sort of energy and left Te'hæra Thorn," Lincoln said.

There was a brief moment of silence. Then, in the distance, a police siren sliced through the quiet evening. Lincoln shifted in his seat.

"I can't go home," he said.

"No," Lea agreed. "As much as I'm sure you want to be with and talk to your parents, going home would complicate things. It would also put them in greater danger."

"Okay, then. How am I going to get Kayleigh back?"

"Lincoln," the older woman said softly, "Getting Kayleigh back is only part of the problem. Emil believed that both you and Kayleigh would be the ones to bring back the de'Malange."

"But they were all cut down," Lincoln said, rising from his seat. "The entire valley is empty. The only de'Malange left is Kafir Rosette and she's in Burnam Tau'roh."

"There are two ways back to de'Na, Lincoln. Traveling through an oak is one."

"But the oaks in Autumn Harbor are just plain oak trees."

Ignoring this comment, Lea continued, "The other way is by using a book that has an activation panel in it."

"*The History of Burnam Tau'roh* had one," Lincoln said.

"Yes."

"But where did it come from? Who put it in the library in the first place?"

"That very question haunted Emil until the day he left."

"Is the book still back in the closet?"

"No. Truman took the book after you left. Fortunately, there is another one."

"The copy they found with me in the boat," Lincoln said.

"Correct," she smiled.

"You have it here?" Lincoln asked, surprised.

"Yes. Now listen carefully. Your only hope of finding Kayleigh is probably with the help of a woman named Mona Tarok. Have you been to the Oak Hotel?"

"Yes. We met her when we first went through."

"Good. Tell her everything that has happened. She's one of the few people you can trust. For some reason Truman trusts her, too. She hears a lot, so there's a good chance she might know something. When you find Kayleigh, the two of you need to find a boy named David Grey. He lives on the coast of the Eastern Sea."

"That's kind of vague," Lincoln said.

"I spent years pouring over that second copy of *The History of Burnam Tau'roh*. The name David Grey appears twice, scribbled among the more cryptic of pages. It's a long shot, but our only lead so far."

"I just want to get Kayleigh back."

"I know. You mustn't give up hope."

A loud knock on the front door of the library caused them both to jump.

"Lea Ruttier?" a muffled voice asked. "I'm Officer White with the Autumn Harbor Police Department. Please unlock this door."

The librarian quickly whispered the location of the book and Lincoln was off.

Another knock at the front door pushed him even faster, up the main stairway, down the main stacks of contemporary literature. Running past unending rows of shelves, he slowed at K and stopped at L. Turning left, he made his way to the end of the aisle and slid to a stop. Grabbing books at random, Lincoln worried that he had misunderstood Ms. Ruttier's directions. Pushing one last book aside, he discovered the concealed panel at the bottom of the shelf. Opening it, he found the second copy of *The History of Burnam Tau'roh*.

The front door below opened. He heard the librarian say in her most innocuous voice, "Hello, Officer. How are you this evening?"

Lincoln turned quickly to the last page of the book and stared at the metallic disc with the small screen in the center— the activation panel. He tapped the tiny menu item marked Burnam Tau'roh. A new menu popped up, this time with three choices: *Oak Hotel*, *Shora Cessyu*, and *Ceca Hebona*.

"Is there anyone here in the library with you this evening, Ma'am?" the officer asked.

If only I had a little more time, Lincoln thought. There are so many questions I never had the chance to ask!

Swallowing hard, he touched the rectangle that said *Oak Hotel*. There was no sound, only a rush of warm static and the sensation of falling at great speed.

Lincoln was gone.

To be continued in…

The Painted

Lighthouse

The Chronicles of

Burnam Tau'roh

Book Two

Pronunciation Guide

Burnam Tau'roh – bur-NAHM TAH-row

de'Na – day-NAH

Kafír Rosette – ka-FEAR roh-SET

Te'hæra Thorn – tuh-HAY-rah THORN

Ka Tolerates – KAH toe-leh-RAH-tays

Kana Hove – kah-nah HOVE

Quercus – KWAIR-kus

de'Malange – day muh-LAHNJ

Mona Tarok – moe-nah TAIR-ok

Kell-Korai – kell kor-EYE

Shora Cessyu – shor-ah say-SOO

Cast of Characters

Kayleigh Lambert – A twelve year-old girl from Autumn Harbor. Kayleigh is on a quest to discover the secrets of her Grandmother's past.

Lincoln Torres – A twelve year-old boy from Autumn Harbor. He and Kayleigh are best friends.

Laura Corwin – Kayleigh's Grandmother.

Lea Ruttier – The Autumn Harbor town librarian.

Mona Tarok – The cook and keeper of the Oak Hotel.

Truman Stitch – The corrupt Mayor of Burnam Tau'roh.

Sheenie Tosh – Truman's sister.

Clyde Manrope – The strange stationmaster who tends Ticket Station IX on the Burnam Tau'roh Eastern Line.

Shipmaster Creek – The proprietor of The Cinema in the forgotten town of Shora Cessyu.

BTEL #3 – A locomotive train that runs on the Burnam Tau'roh Eastern Line.

Kafir Rosette – A mysterious, sentient tree hidden deep in the woods of Burnam Tau'roh.

Emil Corwin – Kayleigh's Grandfather.

Ka Tolerates – An evil tree that inhabits the Valley of the Oaks on Te'hæra Thorn.

Walter Klimczak is the author of *Falling in the Garden* and *This Place Only*, the first two books in the TimeFront series. He lives in Atlanta, Georgia with his wife and three children.